In the desert

Thomas Colton

Contents

Ch. 1: What's Owed

He climbs up from the gulch, scorched dry these past eight years, draggin' his right leg like he don't want nothin' to do with it. The sun shines on his face and I think, he ain't real. Cain't be. No one comes out of that gulch. Not no more.

But unless mirages talk, he is real. This one, he talks, and he says his name is Rordan, but I cain call him Ro on account of the fact that Rordan is kind of a mouthful. The way he says it, I gotta wonder if he means in general, or just fer uneducated common folk livin' on the edge of the desert. People like me.

Two R's in one name ain't exactly a tongue twister. I don't argue the point, though, cuz I'm too caught up on the fact that this man, maybe twenty turns 'round the sun or so, is here at all. And what does he want? That's what I gotta find out. So I say, "Whadaya want?" but he just laughs at me. It's a nice laugh, not meant as belittlin'. Still, I'm annoyed and confused by it. It ain't funny to wanna know what a strange man walkin' up to my porch fifty miles south of nowhere wants. It's downright logical. I cain feel myself edgin' towards Frank, who's restin' against the back of a rickety pillar, the one barely managin' to hold my roof up over the porch. Not yet, Frank, not yet. I gotta use my words to settle this, if I cain.

"I want water," the man, Ro, reports. He cain't seem to stop grinnin' even though this ain't exactly the kind of predicament that would make normal folks happy.

"Water's a need, not a want. Didn't your ma ever teach you the difference?"

Ro laughs again and I take a step closer to Frank, who's still hidin' real good. "I guess that's true. I need water, and I want a place to rest for the night. I'm willing to work for a cool spot out of the sun, and maybe a little food too, if you have any to spare."

"Well, what cain you do?" I gotta ask him, cuz food to spare ain't exactly as common as the dust rollin' into the pastures with every passin' wind. If he wants some, he's gonna have to earn every bite.

"I can do whatever needs doing." His words shake free from his throat like a moth castin' off its cocoon.

Well, I'll be. Desperation exists behind that handsome no-care-in-the-world smile, after all. He's been bakin' in the sun too long. Soon his brain's gonna be all fried up, along with that cornhusk head of his, and he knows it. The fool part of me wants to let him right in, no questions asked, give him a tall glass of water and a bed to sleep on. The rest of me, the part that's almost in reach of Frank, thinks, not so fast.

"Everything needs doin'," I say, and that's true enough. The farm is in shambles as I'm sure this Rordan guy cain see fer himself.

Ro knows he's not gettin' too far with me. He tries fer a different approach. "Do you have a father, or a husband? Is there someone else here I can talk to?"

"The cough got pa and ma years ago," I tell him cuz there ain't no point in pretendin' those people still exist when they don't. "As fer a husband, you see a man worth marryin' anywhere near these parts, you just let me know." I feel like spittin', that's how much I think of them men, boys really, who roam these dusty plains. Ain't no use to them beyond a roll in the hay... and then where does that leave you?

"So... you're all alone here?" That's said with genuine surprise, along with a hint of something behind them blue eyes of his that I cain't quite decipher. I don't like not bein' able to figure things out, especially when the thing that needs figurin' is the motivations of a proper-talkin' stranger.

"Well, until Granddad gets back from his trip," I yank Frank out from behind the post, "it's just me and Frank, here."

I aim Frank at Ro's head, right between them pearly marbles of his, to which he responds with an understandable, "What the hell?" If he was a bit surprised that I'm holdin' my own on this farm, he's downright flabbergasted at the sight of a shotgun being drawn upon his person. He don't seem too familiar with the experience, probably on account of the fact that guns are illegal here on our peaceful little world. "Where did you get that?"

Frank, like everything else 'round here, comes from Granddad, but I don't feel a need to tell this to Ro. I stay silent while Frank and Ro have themselves a starin' competition, and it ain't hard to figure out who's gonna win it.

Ain't but a moment, and Ro looks to his feet. All the excitement he must've felt comin' up to the house thinkin' he could get all his needs and wants taken care of is long gone.

"Please." He shifts all his weight onto his good leg. "Please."

Frank wants to stay locked onto Ro, but I force him down. "You cain get some water in that well there." I point to the pump across the yard, a ways off to his right. "Help yerself."

Ro looks up, spies the well, and then takes his gaze back to meet mine. Rest assured, there ain't nothin' I cain't read in his eyes now. I nod, pleased that we got all that uncertainty out of the way, fer the time bein' at least. "I hope you don't mind goats, cuz after you feed and water 'em, they'll be sharin' their fine accommodations with you." Frank has a big influence on me and he says there ain't no way I'm lettin' this man into my house. No matter that Frank's not much of a conversationalist and I might like someone made of flesh and bones and blue eyes to talk to fer once.

Maybe Ro ain't so good a conversationalist as I thought, though, cuz he turns 'round and starts limpin' toward the water pump without so much as a word.

"My name's May, case you care to know who to direct your thank yous to."

"May." he keeps on hobblin'. "Thank you."

#

I let Ro have his drink. He tries his best to tend the goats, but he's next to worthless. They cain probably do fer themselves better than the care he's providin', but I don't interfere, cuz his half-assed goat tendin's 'bout as much entertainment as I've had since forever.

Eventually, Ro hobbles under the goat shed, sits himself down on some hay and stretches out his bad leg, wincin' all the while. Perched on the front stoop, I'm attemptin' to fight off the heat of the day like a dog itchin' away fleas. Don't matter how much scratchin' I do, it's goin' to keep on with its daily infestation, settin' my skin to boil even in the shade. I rest Frank in my lap and watch. Pretty soon, I cain't take no more of his wincin', so I bring Frank inside and exchange him fer Ma's goat hide medicine bag, worn with time down to a smooth, soft brown. Ma was a healer, or what passes fer one out here.

Ma learned from her own ma, who learned from her pa, and so on. Been healers fer I don't know how many generations, maybe goin' back all the way to the very first folks who came here to colonize this world. Course I got no proof of that, but it's nice to think it's true, that we was always the type of family to lend a hand when it's most needed, even if the needy people might be the secretly dangerous type, hidin' their bad side under a sunburned nose and a boyish grin.

Healin's how my ma met my pa. He grew up right in this very house, the one I've been bustin' my rump tryin' to keep in one piece. Back then, the farm had more neighbors than it does now, but town was still the same distance away – too dang far. Them bein' farmers and havin' to tend to their livestock and fields, Pa had little occasion to go to town, where Ma was livin' with her healer parents. Durin' his once or twice a year excursions into civilization, he had never happened to lay eyes upon my purdy ma. It wasn't until misfortune danced with him while he was patchin' up his leaky roof, causin' him to lose his balance and fall into the shrubbery on the house's south end, that he had occasion to make her acquaintance.

Seein' Pa's leg twisted under him at an odd angle, Granddad had set it himself as best he knew how. By the next morning though, Pa was given over to a fever, and that's when Granddad knew he couldn't heal him all on his own. He'd left right away and the next day he'd returned with my ma. She'd worked her magic on him, knowin' just which tinctures and teas would ease him away from death's door.

When all was said and done, he had a leg that would keep him upright and movin' forward, plus an affection fer my ma that would bring him a joy I can only dream of. It took some convincin' but after a while Ma agreed to move out here so she could be with him. Pa continued to work the fields, and Ma, she made herself known to all the farmin' families here abouts as a midwife and healer. By the time I came along, they was the most lovin', happy couple you could imagine. Pa always said that breakin' his leg was the most fortunate misfortune of his life.

As a little girl, hearin' the story of their meetin' always filled me with wonder, not that they'd found sich love, but cuz I couldn't imagine 'em ever not havin' each other. How could they have grown up as strangers, not even knowin' the other existed? It seemed they was always together, which is probably why Pa didn't live but a few weeks beyond Ma. It's a cruel thing, havin' yer love die still so young and beautiful. Ain't everyone strong enough to keep goin' after that.

Anyways, all of this is to say that I picked up a thing or two in the healin' arts 'fore my ma succumbed. Not much, though. Not enough to cure her of the cough, nor Pa neither. Now I got my own patient, and ain't it strange that it's his leg that's the matter, just like it was with Pa! I gotta pray what I know will be enough to heal what's ailin' him.

I take ma's bag down to the goat pen, shoo them beasts out of the way with a few harsh words, and crouch down in front of Ro.

"You gonna show me it or what?" I ask him.

Ro takes a moment to decide, though I cain't imagine what kind of an 'or what' scenario could be goin' through that purdy head of his that would make him decline my help. He's really and truly out of options at this point.

"I think it's just sprained." He cuffs up his trouser leg slowly, like his leg's gonna come clean off if he ain't careful with it.

I suck in my breath and force myself to stare at that ankle, all hot and red and swollen like a goat's udders a day overdue fer milkin'.

"Just sprained? How long you been walkin' on it like that?"

"A couple of days." Those must've been some awful long days cuz he closes his eyes and leans his head back against the wall of the shed like he's rememberin' every single minute of 'em.

"Ain't good." I scoop up some of the hay from around him, makin' a little pillow out of it, then I raise up his leg as gentle as I cain and rest it on top. Out of ma's pouch comes some balm, left over from the days when there was people 'round to tend to who could benefit from it. It's old, but still, I'm assumin' from its pungent aroma that it'll work just fine. Ro scrunches up his nose so I know he's smelled it too, but he don't say nothin' 'bout it. I put a fair amount on all the parts of his ankle that look to need it.

Ro's blue eyes open while I'm tendin' to him. They rest on me and I try not to notice, try not to care where they travel to as I work on fixin' him up.

"There." I roll his pants back down. "Keep yer leg elevated, like that, and try not to move it. I'll bring some food out to you soon as I cain."

"I've hardly earned it." Does he means the food I promised him or the way I worked my healin' balm over his injured leg? Both, maybe.

"Well, now you owe me." Ma's medicine bag swings from my hip as I stand to leave. "And believe me, I intend to collect."

Ch. 2: The Used-to-Be Fields

Some say that we was chosen, our ancestors, and what they mean is, we're special cuz supposedly, there weren't no one on this world before we got here – no humans, hardly even any animals larger than a tortoise. This world, it was given to us. To our people. No one else. Our folks were from other worlds at one point. And when I say other worlds, I don't mean we got here in no spaceship.

Hundreds of years ago, our pioneers came from alternate realities, if you can believe it. On those worlds, they had all kinds of things – flying cars and tall buildings made of metal. But our folks, we didn't want sich things. The story goes that some fancy scientists called Vitalists took it upon themselves to find a universe that we could call our own. We'd live in peace close to the land in a way that sounds nice on paper, at least.

A better world it was meant to be, though there are others that dispute sich claims, say all that talk of chosen folks and utopian dreams ain't nothin' more than a pack of lies. This ain't no better world – it's a sickly cousin to them other parallel realities at best, and we ain't special cuz we're here.

We're cursed.

I don't praise the gods cuz I'm a supposed chosen one. I don't believe in sich nonsense. But I also don't deny that there's a reason our great-great-however-many-greats-you-wanna-throw-in-there grandparents was brought here to this shriveled up world. It's like they was bein' punished, only they was too dumb to realize it. In fact, from what I've always been told, they thought they was bein' rewarded. A lot of folks still do. Sure, this world has one continent instead of the seven or so most of the known worlds have, but that was all right with them. It's a big continent and what did it matter—one continent or twelve, as long as it was home.

That our pioneers was plunked down on this planet determined to swear off the sophisticated science that made gettin' here possible in the first place always strikes me as ironic. As does the fact that them Vitalist scientists fergot to include in our deluxe package most useful animals sich as, oh I don't know, a gods damn horse fer instance. I mean, if they was givin' us this world all special fer the chosen few, cuz we're so great, why would they refuse us the means of makin' a decent go of it here?

Sure, the rich and powerful pioneers got set up with the best pieces of land out in the Regions, them fertile areas that border the coasts. Everyone else? We been hard scramblin' since the day we arrived here, even 'fore the desert started spreadin'. They gone and put a bunch of technology-dependent folks back on the land, and them folks said that was exactly what they wanted, sure. To live simple. But I gotta wonder if they changed their tune after the first season gone by without a lot to show fer it. And without so much as a horse with which to attempt their escape.

Not that there was somewheres to escape to by then....

We got plunked down in this plane, this sorry excuse for a reality, but it seems purdy likely the ones doin' the plunkin' returned to their cushy world and fergot about us. We ain't heard of no off-worlders visitin', at least. They just left and said good riddance on their way out. And what did we know about openin' a way from this world back to theirs? Nothin' it seems, cuz here we sit in the swelterin' sun, turnin' from plum to prune by the bushel.

Chosen ones my ass.

I'm ruminatin' over all this as I put Ro's dinner together—a potato, a couple wilted carrots and a precious square of cheese. Ro accepts my humble offerings, sich as they are, lickin' his plate clean like it's the best thing he ever tasted. I take his plate back up to the house, and eat my own dinner with no one but Frank and a sunset fer companionship. They're quiet, but loyal. I've grown accustomed to the silence since the trip Granddad took to town when supplies ran low. The trip he ain't come back from.

I bring my visitor an old crocheted blanket, cuz it gits mighty cold in the desert after the sun dips away. But he's already asleep, Nessie and Reba curled up next to him, snorin' goat snores and dreamin' goat dreams. Them goats probably give him all the warmth he needs, but I lay the blanket on him anyway 'fore headin' up to bed.

By the time I get down there in the mornin', Ro is already up, makin' ready with the stuff in his pack. A bunch of thin books are shoved into a side pocket. All of 'em look the same, but I cain't tell fer sure cuz he closes it up 'fore I cain give 'em a proper look. My blanket's neatly folded, restin' on the fence.

"What you doin'?" Poor boy, he nearly jumps out of his skin at the sound of my voice. "I thought I told you to stay off that leg."

Ro slings his pack onto his shoulder and flashes me with that cocky smile of his. "I thought I'd taken enough of the goat's hospitality. And your own, of course, May."

"You got somewheres you need to be 'fore the next full moon?" One hand on my hip, the other holdin' onto the milkin' pail, and this glare of mine means business. "Cuz yer not likely to get there on that ankle. You got some healin' to do first."

Ro's smile falls away but his eyes hold steady. They've been lookin' at me, straight and true since I surprised him by my presence in his hay bale hotel. "Injury or not, May, I think I better keep going."

"And I'm sayin' you cain't, even if you wanna." I scoot a stool out of the corner of the shed and coax Reba over with a bit of grain. "Ain't nothin' but desert fer hundreds of miles south of here, and if I'm not mistaken, that's the direction yer headin'."

Ro drops his bag onto the ground, his expression turned right serious. "How do you know in what direction I'm heading?"

"Cuz it's obvious, fool," I give Reba a pat and get to yankin'. A thin stream of warm milky heaven graces the bottom of my bucket. "You came up through the gulch. Now that's to the west, and it's the only thing to the west fer a long ways— A mighty inhospitable place fer travelers since the creek done dried up way back when. So there ain't a good reason to show up here from that direction 'cept if you was forced to go through there cuz you was tryin' to circumvent something. Something you wanted to avoid. Say, a town with people in it. Nearest town's directly north of here, so you ain't goin' there. You could be headed east, I suppose, but there's an officer's camp in that direction and something tells me that's the last place you wanna find yerself anywheres near. That leaves south. Ain't nothin' south, which I'm thinkin' suits you just fine. No people, no nothin'. Perfect place to get lost in. Course, it's a perfect place to die in too."

"I don't intend to die." He walks 'round to my side of Reba, watchin' me work breakfast out of a scruffy underfed goat, all the while shufflin' weight back and forth 'tween his legs, but mainly onto the one that actually works. There's uncertainty 'tween us again, only this time, it's all on his side. He didn't think I'd figure him out so easy. Makes him rightly nervous.

"Most people don't intend to die, but they still end up doin' it, don't they?" I keep at my work till Reba's gone run dry. "Next up." I vacate my seat and lead Nessie over fer her turn.

Ro stands in the one place the eastern light cain't reach. The far corner of the shed hides his face. It's like he don't wanna be seen all of a sudden.

"I said, 'next up.'" I gesture toward the stool. "You do want breakfast 'fore you go traipsin' off to your certain demise in the great southern wasteland, don't you?"

"You want me to do that?" He takes a step out of the gloom and his face gets back all its fine features. But he don't sit. Nessie bleats, tosses her head from side to side like, git it over already, why don't you.

"It's just a gods damn goat, Rordan," I make sure to pronounce his name all proper-like, with both the R's in their places and the O all nice and long. "Come on, don't be shy."

Nessie's actually a lot cagier than Reba, and I saved her fer him on purpose, cuz ain't nothin' more fulfillin' than watchin' someone who's never done milkin' before have an ornery goat put him in his place. Naturally, Nessie has to go and disappoint me in my petty endeavors. Ro talks real sweet to her, pets her gentle, then sets to milkin'. He must have been studyin' me real hard cuz he's awkward at first, but only at first. It takes him a little long, but he does it. He milks Nessie and she don't try to nip at him not once.

"Well, well, looks like you made a friend."

"I hope you're referring to yourself." He's all quiet, bashful even, as he wipes his hands on the front of his trousers.

I snort. "Hope you don't think you cain win favors with me that easy." Swishin' the bucket 'round, I take account of how much we got. "Not bad."

Actually, it is bad. The girls don't give much these days. I keep turnin' my mind from the thought that someday, they won't give at all. And then, like Janie and Selma and Beryl, and all the chickens too, I'll have to see them on their way to their final restin' spot—the bottom of Grandma Stebbin's copper soup kettle.

I pour Ro's share into a jar brought down from the house fer just this occasion, and then I deliver my own lot, straight back into my throat. Ro looks at his breakfast dubiously.

"Is this all that you—I mean, is this your usual..." He twists the jar in his hands as if the motion's gonna magically fill it up. I cain tell what he's tryin' to avoid askin'. He don't wanna be rude, but the fact that he said anything at all makes him too late fer that particular want.

"I'm glad to have this." My jaw's set firm all of a sudden. "Folks 'round here appreciate what they got."

"Sorry." If I'm to judge by the flush of his cheeks, I'd say he really is. He drinks his milk and then his eyes turn back to me. This time, I have to wrestle with myself, not to feel uncomfortable under his stare. What's he see anyway? A girl with wild black curls flyin' out of her head in any direction they please, dressed in her ma's baggy old coveralls, which, try as they might, still cain't hid her scraggly arms and beanpole body. No one eats proper here. That's just the way of it and has been fer a long while. We all look like the wind might tip us over, a fact I never gave much thought to, until this Ro guy comes through and gives me the once over.

Well it don't matter. He sees what he sees. And from the amount of lookin' he's been doin', he cain't be too repulsed by me.

"I know I'm quite the desert beauty, but if you don't stop yer gawkin', I'm goin' to have to start chargin' you." I grab Ro's emptied cup back from him and put it in my bucket so I cain take it to the pump fer washin'. "And I ain't sure you've got the kind of payment I'm interested in."

His smile comes back just enough for his eyes to alight. "Don't be so sure."

I convince Ro to put off his futile journey, at least another few days. It's either stay here and put up with me and my paltry meals, or go and put up with no meals at all and a death by desert. Even on two good feet, most people ain't stupid enough to venture through that particular stretch of dust. He's just askin' fer it if he don't take my advice. I'm surprised to say, he finally does. He must be desperate if he's gonna listen to me cuz, who am I to him really? Course, the better questions is, who is he?

I already know he must come from one of the Regions. Not the big middle part we're standin' in now, but one of the outlier areas that circle us, on the rim of the continent. There's more than one season aside from Dry in the Regions and that means you don't gotta squeeze life outa death every day the way you do here. The Regions got their own way of livin', and as far as I cain tell, they maintain that way by keepin' the rest of us in our place.

After our hearty breakfast, I make him haul water to the vegetable patch and use the opportunity to question him.

"Where you appear from, anyways?" I watch as he draws water up out of the ground.

"I'm from the city," is all he says.

"Well, no shit, yer from the city. I guess what I mean to say is, what's a city dweller like yerself doin' here? We ain't exactly on the map. And yer kind don't usually like to associate themselves with me and mine."

"My kind?" he peers at me real strange, like I've truly offended him. "Just what is my kind?"

"Don't give me that, Rordan. You know what I mean. Everyone knows there're only two types of people on this gods' forsaken planet. Them that's lucky, and them that ain't. You was born from the lucky ones, and I was born-well?" I sweep my hand 'round to indicate my surroundings, "Here. Unluckyville. I ain't complainin', though."

"No," he laughs, "you ain't complainin'."

"What, now you gonna make fun of how I talk? Is that it? You think cuz the way I talk, I must be unintelligent, don't you?"

"I didn't say that." All the sudden, the water stops gittin' pumped and there he is standing with that offended expression sappin' his good looks again.

"I talk this way cuz this is how people does it here. Probably the first people in these parts talked real similar, so it just goes to follow. Ain't nothin' unintelligent about it. You wanna talk about not smart, how about decidin' what's proper and stickin' to it, even if it makes no sense. Ain't that what you and your kind are all about? Rules, rules, and more rules. All to make you out as bein' more important, better than the rest of us. Now that's good justification fer you to go on with your lucky lives, and leave the rest of us here in the desert to dry up and die. At least then, our bad luck cain't rub off on you."

Ro shakes his head, wipes the sweat from his brow and sets his eyes to the horizon."I like the way you talk, May. And as for smarts, I'd be foolish to even consider competing with you. I don't deny that my kind, as you put it, is guilty of thinking the way you just mentioned, maybe worse. But let me ask you this, if I was so lucky, if things were as wonderful in the Regions as you seem to assume, why am I out here, in your corner of nowhere, sleeping in a goat shed, and taking your unjust criticism?"

Well, now, that is something to ponder. Still, he ain't given me the answers I'm lookin' fer. Each of us lifts a bucket and we haul water over to my sorry excuse fer a garden. "Look, Rordan, there's only so many reasons why someone like you would walk through that gulch and end up on my farm. I know you got the law after you, and I ain't askin' you to tell me why."

"So you really don't want to know?"

"Oh I wanna know. Fact, I'm dyin' of curiosity. What I mean is, you tellin' me ain't a condition of yer stay here. I already offered my hospitality, and I ain't as interested in yer crimes as I am in yer character. You've already convinced Nessie that yer all right, but you ain't convinced me. Not yet. So whatever you cain do to plead yer case, best you go ahead."

"And what do I get, if I convince you I'm actually an upstanding citizen, that this running from the law is all just the result of a big misunderstanding?"

"You git a kick to that bum ankle of yers fer lyin' to me."

He raises his eyebrows. "Fine, then. What if instead I give you the truth, you believe it, and what's more, you like me better for it. What then?"

"Another measly meal comes yer way." I empty my bucket and toss it to the ground. "Only you cain have it at the kitchen table like civilized folk, and you cain enjoy a night's rest without breathin' in goat droppings."

Ro wobbles a bit as he waters the dust. It's already hotter than hot out and I shouldn't be encouragin' him to walk on that leg, so I offer him the slightly less hot shade of the porch. He sets himself in a chair and puts his sore leg up on the railing. Elevated, just like I told him. He looks out toward the north, where town is, then gives me one of his customary deep stares 'fore he opens his mouth.

"If you're sure, May, then here goes."

Ch. 3: Partygoers' Luck

R o sleeps in Granddad's bed that night, in the loft that looks down onto the kitchen. I nestle in my own bed, right below that loft. He sleeps real quiet-like—so quiet, I cain almost convince myself he ain't even there. But my own breath catches when I do that. I want him to be there but I ain't at peace with that. I been alone long enough that I should be used to it by now. So how come I like havin' Ro 'round so much? It shouldn't matter whether he comes or goes, but I'm honestly glad he's here now, whether it's because of what he told me out on the porch today, or in spite of it—I'm not sure which.

Ro ain't killed no one. He tells me that first off and seems keen on me believin' it, if nothin' else. He adds in that he ain't no threat to me. He'd sooner slit his own wrists than do me harm.

"That's pretty dramatic," I tell him. Leadin' with a declaration of suicide should he act dishonorable towards me—he certainly has a flair fer tale tellin'. So I say, "Go on and git to the rest of the story."

He's from the capital city, which is what I suspected. Grew up there all his life near the city's soarin' spires. And also like I thought, his life is lucky, right from the start. He's privileged and never wants fer nothin'.

He got him a good childhood... happy. Durin' his young days, he rarely sees the parts of his city where the poor wretches live—the slums where folks are driven in order to escape their fruitless farms 'fore they get swallowed up by the desert. The Regions don't take in common folk as a rule, but it turns out the capital city makes an exception. Likes to show how merciful it is, lettin' desperate folk from inferior stock feed off its leftovers, and even gives a few of those folk employment of the toilet cleanin' variety.

I believe Ro has a toilet cleaner at his own fine house, but the only time he ever glimpses at where that woman comes from is when he leaves the city each summer to go on what he calls a wilderness expedition. That's where, if you cain believe it, people actually pretend to be homeless and without all their city conveniences. They make fun times out of survivin' off the land, till it tires 'em out, at which point they go back to their food-brought-on-a-platter-every-mornin' lives once more.

I cain't quite wrap my head 'round this, that his kind have to play at survival, that it don't just come natural from day to day gettin' by. They still gotta find a way to pretend once a year when the weather is nice and all the forest berries are in season. Must be rough. It do explain how he managed to git this far from the capital, across hundreds and hundreds of miles of harsh land, not a toilet cleaner in sight, all without expirin'. Pretend survival's paid off fer him, and I gotta remember that. Best I don't discount Ro as fast as I was first inclined to.

Anyways, goin' on these wilderness expeditions means travelin' from its pristine luck-filled center through the dangerous parts of town, where all the folks like me git stuck and evidently stay stuck till the day they die. But he tries his best not to see 'em, tries his best to ignore their stench, to ferget their sufferin'. He's a kid, so he cain push his mind in other directions, but not entirely. Somewhere at the back of his head, he notes their sufferin' and stores it fer future reference, and it's so well hidden, he don't even know this knowledge exists in himself till years later.

Eventually, the campin' trips stop and the upper education starts. College. That's something they got in the Regions, along with schools in general. Ro is on his way to becomin' a journalist. He learns all about turnin' facts into a good story, as his own life facts spelled out fer me in one hotter-than-hot afternoon stand in testament of. He gits apprenticed to a man who teaches him how to set type, how to put thoughts on a piece of paper and make 'em stick there. Ro believes he'll finish school and then work with this teacher till that teacher retires, which is what wealthy folks git to do 'fore they die, stead of constant work bein' the cause of their demise. After that, he'll take over, writin' government-approved news stories, printin' papers, gittin' people to read what he wrote. Well, this end up comin' to fruition, just not nearly the way he imagines it.

A few months into his first year of college, Ro meets up with a fellow student, name of Stuart. Him and Stuart started a real friendship, which includes drinkin' what he refers to as copious amounts of liquor. Now, a thing you gotta know about the Regions is that they don't take kindly to alcohol consumption. So this liquor drinkin' takes place where the authorities ain't bound to care overly much about it—at an underground tavern in the poor part of town.

Time and time again, Ro and Stuart make their way to their favorite spot, a hole in the wall called Mattie's, and it don't take long fer Ro to start seein', I mean really seein', what's 'round him. That exposure from his childhood starts creepin' out of his subtle mind into his not-so-subtle mind and he's back to bein' a spectator in the middle of a field growin' up sufferin' like it's a fertile vineyard. Only now, he ain't just passin' through the fields, he's there to squeeze juice from them grapes.

It don't take long fer his emotions to get all mixed up. Here he is, comin' to a place most people hope to escape, and he's there to recreate, like he's back on a wilderness expedition, playin' at something everyone else considers the hardest form of hard labor. It makes him feel real bad, and after a while, he cain't stop his bad feelin' from spillin' over.

One night, several bottles already drained, he tells Stuart these here poor parts of town is startin' to weigh on him. Something's not right, he says to his friend. Something's not fair.

He expects... I don't know... a pep talk from Stuart, I suppose. Stuart's every bit as lucky in his life as Ro is in his own. He'll probably slap Ro on the back, buy him another drink, and tell him not to worry about these sorry saps beggin' on the tavern's threshold. Don't mind the shoeless children, or their doped-up parents. Just look at 'em. They ain't us, he'll say to Ro. They deserve to live this way.

Well, Stuart don't say or do none of those things, 'cept he really does slap Ro on the back. He smiles as he tells Ro, "Finally. I've been wondering when you were going to come around." Then he hops out of his chair and leads Ro back behind the bar, ignorin' the Employees Only sign. Stuart pushes open a door and it turns out, there's a back room to Mattie's Tavern. Ro's jaw nearly hits the floor at what awaits him in that room. Papers and books and a printing press, and mixed up with all of that, folks, lucky and unlucky, all workin' together. Fer what? Well, the word Stuart uses is, "justice."

Turns out, their printer had up and got herself arrested a few weeks back. "So," Stuart says, "I need you to take over. You in?"

Ro wouldn't be spendin' tonight up in Granddad's bed if he'd declined Stuart's offer, but of course, he says yes. He starts out printin' fliers about rallies and organizational meetings, tryin' to convince the capital's poor to come together. These sorts of activities, in which poor folks try to figure out how to get themselves not poor, ain't even close to bein' acceptable in the eyes of the law. Ro knows he'll be in trouble if it's found out he's usin' his skills to spread the message that people don't just have to mistake misery fer a death sentence. He believes things cain change, and he calculates his personal risk based on that believe.

This goes on fer a while, him almost gittin' caught on three separate occasions. They have to move the underground press to different locals to keep it secret. One time, they don't beat the law and all their stuff gits burned up and two of their workers git arrested. But they persist, none-the-less.

One night, him and Stuart are talkin' with this commoner, name of Amos. Amos is a refugee, newly arrived from the heart of the Desert and he says to 'em, "Fer all of yer learnin', it's funny how none of yous know what all of us desert dwellers have accepted as true fer years."

And Stuart and Ro are like, "Tell us, Amos. We don't wanna be stupid city boys no more." Course they say it more proper than that, but anyways, Amos responds, "Well, the desert, it's spreadin'."

"Yeah, yeah." They shake their heads. "We know all about desertification."

"Yes, but no." Amos shakes his head back at 'em. "This ain't something that cain be reversed. The situation seems to be permanent. It just stopped rainin' at the center of the world and the no rain is spreadin' itself out. Pretty soon, it's gonna be a desert here too. All us refugees know it, cuz we've lived through our houses and our towns goin' under the sands, but you folks in the Regions, you've turned a blind eye so that you could enjoy the party fer another hour or two. But the party's gotta end at some point."

The two lucky boys don't know what to say to that. Everything' they was doin', it has to seem pretty futile in light of Amos' revelations.

"May," Ro breaks from his storytelling. "That's why you're wrong about lucky and unlucky. It doesn't matter if you're living on a goat farm east of a dried up gulch, or in a fancy house surrounded by the capital's luxury. Sooner or later, luck's going to run out for every single one of us."

I cain barely breathe from takin' all this in. My eyes glisten at the corners, but I refuse to cry. Ro looks a mite apologetic, layin' all this on me, but he's got a story to finish, so he keeps goin'.

What Amos said, Ro takes to heart. He don't bury it back in his mind like he did the sufferin' of the refugees back when he was a boy. Till this point, the underground press has acted to git information out to the common poor. But him and Stuart agree that it's time to inform the genteel population of the followin'—their perfect little world ain't nothin' but a dream nearly come to an end.

So, they git to work, writin' up a booklet detailin' the desert's spread over the years, and estimatin' how long it'll take to reach the Regions. They don't just take Amos' word fer it, neither. They talk to dozens of refugees from all over the land, ask 'em when they left their homes, what year the desert reached 'em, how fast the dust storms traveled. So on and so forth. This helps 'em form what they feel is a fairly accurate depiction of the continent's process of desertification. And it confirms Amos' statement in a most alarmin' way—it won't be but a few years 'fore the luck of their kind takes a turn fer the worse.

The three of 'em, Amos, Ro, and Stuart, write up their findings and Ro gits to printin'. They start with five hundred copies, which don't maybe seem like a lot, but it's enough to fuel the flames. 'Fore long, their booklet, Why the Spread of the Desert Should Matter to You, is the talk of the town. People pass their copies 'round, speculating as to its truthfulness. It don't take more than a month or two fer them to start questionin' their leaders.

This ain't no poor folks' rally Ro and his friends are plannin'. It's a whole renovation of society. They want the government to wise up and tell the truth fer once, but the government—they're still hostin' their party, and they ain't wantin' to go home and deal with their hangovers just yet. They like keepin' folks in the dark, thank you very much, and they don't want no one to listen to these lies, as they call 'em. As you'd expect, this is when the law comes down on Ro's little band of rebels.

One evening, Ro is on his way to the latest location of the press. He's figurin' to start printin' another run of booklets and is real excited about the prospect, thinkin' of the stirrin' the first run did within the lucky parts of the city. Up ahead, he spies smoke, and that ain't good. Soon as he sees it, he knows the press's been compromised, which means they're goin' to have to start over with all new equipment and supplies, yet again.

Only it's worse than that.

Just as he's contemplatin' how close he cain get to the fire without drawin' attention to himself, one of his fellow lucky conspirators, a woman named Breanna, comes hurryin' 'round the corner, holdin' her arm against herself, soot covered and grey tears streamin' down her face.

"They're burning us all," she cries, and Ro thinks she must be out of her mind, but no, she's just statin' a simple fact. Her singed hair's the only proof she needs. She says the law came, waited till they knew there was people inside the press room, sealed the doors shut, and set the place on fire. Breanna managed to break through a boarded up window, but the wall she climbed through collapsed right after her exit. "They're all dead, Ro. Gods, they're all dead."

All dead means fourteen good people, includin' Amos. And it would have been Ro too if he'd shown up a half hour earlier. Ro heads back to the lucky zone that night, heartbroken, and directionless. What's he gonna do now? He cain't quit, and yet, look what his friends got fer their efforts. Cain he put others at risk that way again? He feels responsible, seein' as he's a decent person who thinks heavily upon these sorts of things. But he ain't the one who should be carryin' this burden, as he soon finds out.

Stuart waits fer him by his house, practically scares Ro out of his skin when he calls Ro's name and invites him into the alley to speak.

"You've got to leave the city." Stuart grips Ro's shirt. His eyes are wild. Frantic. "They'll be here soon, Rordan. You'll never breathe air outside a prison cell again if they catch you."

"What?" Ro's eyes dart to and fro. "How do they even know I'm involved? And Stuart, how do you know they're on to me?"

Stuart, he cain't hide his guilt. He don't even need to say one more gods damn word.

"You sold us out," Ro just cain't believe it. Stuart's the one who brought him in, made him a part of this. He thought his friend was tried and true. "Amos and the others are dead because of you."

Stuart hangs his head, but Ro makes him explain himself. "I had no choice," Stuart claims. "They found out I'd funded the first run. Said they'd pin it on my father. He'd be arrested, maybe even executed, and our family would be ruined."

So there you have it. Fer all of Stuart's grand ideals, when it looked like his own good times were over, he let every well-intended notion slip away. One more dance at the party fer Stuart, but the jig is up fer everyone else.

"I tried to buy you some time." Stuart's shakin' now, but he manages to smile. He truly believes if he cain git Ro to safety, it will make up fer their dead companions, fer the dismantling of their press, fer the end to their quest to enlighten the world. "I told them you were drinking at Mattie's tonight. They'll check there first before coming here."

Ro has just enough time to pack his bag, into which he slips his last ten copies of Why the spread of the Desert Should Matter to You. His parents and his little brother are asleep. He don't wake them to say goodbye and he don't leave a note. He cain barely keep movin' when he thinks of the grief he's 'bout to cause 'em. By the time he gits back out of his house, Stuart's gone, which is just as well, considerin' he never wants to catch sight of that traitor's sorry face ever again.

Ro is only a block away when a whole charge of lawfolk come up from the opposite direction. He hides himself and listens to the rhythmic stomping of their boots as they march towards his house. Soon they're at his stoop yellin', beatin' on his front door, and then there's only the poundin' of his own feet, runnin' away from the law, away from his family, from his life, lucky, unlucky, lucky, unlucky. I imagine, the distinction 'tween the two don't carry much weight fer him no more.

He leaves the city, heads east, stickin' to the Regions, but this ain't safe. Too many lawfolk in the Regions, and too many folks of the law—people who would turn him over soon as they figured out who he is. And he's got the proof of himself right there in his bag. Ten copies of his book. Ten reminders of who he wants to be, not who he was born to be. It's a terrible risk, keepin' them books with him, but he does it anyways. He don't wanna die, he wants to find a new place to set his principles flyin' out into the greater world again. But if he is caught, he ain't gonna turn coward like Stuart did. Those booklets are his insurance that his sense of self won't vanish along with everything else he's lost.

Despite the hardships he faces, Ro endures. He keeps himself fed, upright, and movin'. Several times he almost succumbs to despair, but he just has to believe in himself, believe that he survived and escaped so he could continue his mission. He heads through the Northern Region, then gits to thinkin' that he ain't doin' his mission no good if he cain't face the desert—learn what it's like firsthand. If he cain't brave it, then he'll never be anything more than a hypocrite, and a hypocrite's what Stuart is. That comparison turns his stomach and spurs him on.

'Fore he cain attempt the desert, he needs supplies, a map, knowledge of water sources. So he does what he's avoided doin' till this point. He enters a small town situated not far from where the prosperity of the Regions leaves off fer the plight of the destitute.

He tries to make like he's a local of sorts, just travelin' from another town somewheres in the vicinity. Ain't no trouble comes his way at first, and he gathers the things he needs. He even gits directions to the house of an old desert trader who should be able to clue him in as to where he cain fill up with water on his way south. As he passes the shops on the main lane, he spies the weekly paper in a store window.

How could he not stop and read that headline? How could he not stand there and stare at the article, the news, sent on the wings of a courier bird, straight out of the capital:

Spread of the Desert Revealed as Hoax

Son of Disgraced Business Man Funding Sham Commits Suicide

Co-conspirator Still At Large

"Well, I'll be damned." I cain't control my loose lips when Ro tells me this part. "They pinned it on Stuart's father anyways, even after he turned rat on you."

That is surely what happened, and Stuart, if the paper cain be believed, paid fer his betrayal by guzzlin' a bottle of poison.

There's a line-drawin' of Stuart in that paper, a real good likeness of him, Ro says, and right next to his likeness is one of Ro. It's a sketch his parents had done by a notable artist only a few months past, and it's like lookin' in a mirror. Anyone who reads this paper and notes an unfamiliar man walkin' down their lane is gonna know Ro and this co-conspirator are one and the same.

Shakin' himself free of this realization, Ro resists the urge to flee from town right then and there and carries on with his plan to seek out the trader. He cain't get too far in the desert without the trader's advice and he knows it. But it's still a gamble. One of them shopkeepers may have already identified him, and if they didn't, this trader guy might. He don't got nobody he cain trust, but that's the thing about bein' desperate—you either decide to go ahead with yer sorry excuse fer a plan, or you give up and lay right down in the lane and wait fer the law to descend.

Ro went on ahead. He met with the trader, got the information he needed, and struck out into the wastelands just as soon as he could.

Ever since then, he's had the law on his tail, so someone back at that town must surely have given him up. The desert turns out to be every bit as harsh as he'd been told, and then some, but he lets that spark him on, lets his anguish dry up like the sands at his feet.

"Sand?" I gotta correct him on this point, though technically, I guess in certain places, it cain rightly be called that. "Sand's fer beaches. What we got here is dust—all that's left of the people and things in this world that git swept away. Dirt and skin and ash and bones. Soon there ain't gonna be nothin' but one big ball of dust circlin' the sun."

"Well," he goes on, "The dust, the desert, whatever. It doesn't scare me. I mean, I know it's awful."

"Ain't no doubt 'bout that." I nod, letting him continue with his thoughts.

The dust and Ro, they come to an understanding. He brings his stories with him into that desolate land, asleep in its fallow state and assumed to be dead ferever. He brings his truths, and in exchange fer not killin' him, these truths of his wake the desert's spirit, give it a soul, make it something less monstrous, something that's just tryin' to survive, just tryin' to spread itself, find a new homeland.

That's a curious way of lookin' at it and I tell him so, cuz if he's gonna make the desert into a livin' creature, then what it is is a pest, a parasite that won't be satiated till its host gives up the ghost. And ain't we so lucky that they plopped our ancestors down on this doomed world of ours, only to watch it eaten by Ro's spirit of the wilds, a parasite of monstrous proportions if ever there was one.

Ro, he walks across the desert and it wakes under the feel of his feet and it don't take him down, not even when he crosses that gulch, the one filled with the bleached bones of those that tried to pass that way before him. Then it leads him to my doorstep, which he claims to be happy 'bout.

"If you got any sway with the desert, Rordan, maybe you could add my name to its list of people to spare." Not that he cain. This happens sometimes—the desert takin' a man's sanity along with his hydration. What's alarmin' is how sane Ro appears to be when he speaks of the desert, like it's been a better friend to him than most of the people in his life.

#

It's been nearly six months since he left the capital, and still, he ain't found a place to resettle. He don't know how he's gonna spread the word and how even if he finds a way, he cain convince people that we're our own worst enemies, that lies and betrayals and a hunger fer power are all greater evils than the spread of the desert. If we done away with all that, we might find a way to work together to solve our problems. He don't know how he cain accomplish gettin' out to the world everything' that's in his mind.

"Cain I see it, yer booklet?" I bite my lip. I don't know why should I be afraid he'll say no, but I am.

He shifts his weight, lookin' uncomfortable.

"Look here, Rordan. My pa taught me how to read, so you don't gotta worry 'bout me lookin' at it wrong side up or nothin'." I suspect them people in the Regions would be real surprised to know how many of us common folks got some book learnin' in us. Not the kind of book learnin' you git from school, since as I already mentioned, we don't got too many of those, but the kind that determined parents passed down to their offspring, to make sure the next generation ain't completely unversed in the old ways.

"It's not that. I—I haven't shown it to anyone since leaving the city. I haven't even looked at a copy myself."

"Well then, it's 'bout time."

Ro nods, pulls one of the booklets out of his bag, hands it over.

I flip through the first few pages, and then git to readin'. It's everything he told me it would be. All the data he gathered, the stories he documented from desert dwellers. It's all there. Plain as cain be that we got us a global situation on our hands. He watches me as I read, but I don't let that fact rush me. I ain't the fastest reader in the world, but I read real thorough and I remember the words I take in.

When I finish, which don't take too long cuz it's a booklet, only twenty-six pages and there's charts and graphs and whatnot, I hand it back to him.

"Dinner's in an hour." I stand up and head to the door. "Make sure you wash up good at the pump and leave yer boots on the porch. Don't need no more dust inside my house."

Ch. 4: On This Way Forever

My full name is May June Stebbins.

Yeah, I know.

If you thought, guess yer parents couldn't decide on a month, you'd be right. Ma wanted to name me May. Pa preferred June. They never been ones to bicker fer too long, so May June I became. That solved that argument, but Granddad always joked it was a good thing he didn't insist I be called July. Rordan's got nothin' on May June July Stebbins in the mouthful department. The funny thing is, no one thought to name me after the month in which I was born, and I think April's a perfectly acceptable name.

Ro laughs when I tell him 'bout how my name came to be. He says his full name is Rordan Bennett Farnes, which I tell him is a nice name, but not so excitin' as mine, seein' as though it don't got a joke built into it. I'm proud of my name and the story associated with it, and since he spent the afternoon revealin' everything about himself, I figured it's only fair to divulge a few of my own true facts. Turns out, Ro is as curious 'bout me as I am 'bout him. "What you see is what you git," I say to him.

"If only you meant that literally, I'd be a very happy man tonight." Ro grins.

"Now, just what are you implyin', Rordan?" I give him my don't-mess-with-me look, even though on the inside, I ain't totally put off by his flirtations.

"I'm not implying anything, May June Stebbins. I'm saying outright, that you are so beautiful, I couldn't believe you were real when I first saw you standing on your porch."

That's funny, cuz I thought the exact same thing 'bout him. Well, purdy much.

Ro's eyes twinkle. "After everything I'd been through, and so many months avoiding everyone, I suppose I thought I'd be alone forever. But there you were, like the desert knew you were exactly who I needed and it brought me to you. Like you were a gift."

"I ain't no gift," I say quick, cuz what's he thinkin', speakin' like I'm something to be traded 'tween himself and his desert buddy. "But still, thank you fer the compliment, I suppose."

This conversation is takin' place over the dinner table, and he's right across from me, his bad leg situated on a spare chair. He reaches his hand over like he's gonna grab onto mine, then pulls it back. "I don't want you to think I'm trying to take advantage."

"I think you won't have that opportunity. Now I believe it was you who mentioned that I had nothin' to fear from you, Rordan. I don't have to bring Frank back out to prove that point, do I?"

Ro sits back, and he's smilin' but also not smilin' in that way of his that shows mixed emotions.

I should be nicer to him. I should let him grab my hand, and I won't lie, I'm dyin' to taste them lips, to find out what his body looks like under my pa's button-up shirt. I ain't been overly particular with them no-good boys that run the dust up 'round here. I've had my share of fun. But Ro ain't just 'bout fun. He's something more, and I ain't ready to explore what that something more actually is. Cuz won't he be gone in a few days, once his ankle heals up? I cain't be bleedin' my heart out at his absence. I've got plenty of people I bleed over already.

Which leads me to a change in conversation. "My Granddad liked to tell stories, just like you. Well, they weren't based on facts, as far as I cain tell, but they were still nice to listen to. Used to tell me this one passed down from our ancestors 'bout a man who was cursed. He turned into a beast, all ugly and whatnot. And only if he could git a woman to fall in love with him -- furry face, horns, and all -- without tellin' her about the curse, could the spell be undone."

"Did he find someone like that?"

"Granddad says he did. Says there was this young maiden, lovely as the stars, and she had sich a kind heart, she could see beyond the surface, see him fer who he was, and she loved him fer it. Well, that broke the spell and then she had herself not only a brave, noble, and rich man, but a handsome one too. They got married and lived, as Granddad put it, happily ever after."

"Sounds nice."

"Don't it though?" I sigh. "Sometimes I wish I could live in one of Granddad's fairytales."

"May." Ro cocks his head slightly. "What happened to your Grand-father?"

"I told you, he went to town to git supplies."

"How long ago was that?"

"Three months." Ro looks at me sharp, so I add real quick, "But that don't mean he ain't comin' back."

"Oh, May." Ro frowns, and now we got ourselves a new under-standin'. Cuz he knows I know there's a bigger chance the desert will stop its spread than that old man will appear back on the farm.

Still, the last thing I need is his pity. Truth is, Granddad wasn't all about storytellin' and parentin' orphaned girls. He never was one fer keepin' things up, unless it was his bar tab. I've been runnin' this place since I was fourteen, and don't it show? Sure, if he was sober enough, Granddad might be relied upon to fix a broken board in the fence or help me plow our last remainin' semi-productive field. But spots of sobriety didn't come his way too often.

I tell this all to Ro, maybe not in so many words, but he gits the message. Granddad's a drunk, and he either abandoned me here cuz he didn't wanna deal with the farm no more, or he got himself so inebriated in town that something bad happened. I'm mainly thinkin' it's the latter even though that means he's probably dead. I just cain't bear the notion that he'd leave me of his own free will.

"I did go lookin' fer him, 'bout a week after he left," I admit to Ro. "People in town said they'd seen him, but no one knew what had happened to him. The bartender mentioned that Granddad had warmed a stool some nights passed, but he stumbled out into the street at closin' time and that's all he knows."

"Have you tried to find him since then?"

"No I ain't. I almost lost everything' lookin' fer him the first time." The scorn I been harborin' fer Granddad pours right out of me through my bitter words. "It took me a day to walk to town. I spent the night there and didn't git back till the next evening. Two days I'm gone and when I git back, I'm down two goats. Seems some wild beast carried off a couple of 'em. Reba and Nessie were in sorry shape, too. So I cain't go lookin' fer my good-fer-nothin' Granddad again. If I leave this place, I might as well never come back cuz the girls won't make it without me and Frank to watch over 'em. And I won't make it without the girls. See the conundrum I'm in?"

I rest my elbows on the table and hold my head up with my palms.

Ro mimics me so we got our faces no more than a foot a part. "I do see, May. I do. You can't go on this way forever."

"Like I got a choice? Ain't no stellar prospects waitin' fer me out there in the world. This farm is all I have, sich as it is."

"But it can't last, May."

"No it cain't and it won't, but the way you say it, neither will the world. The only comfort I take from yer dire predictions is that I'll already be in my grave 'fore the end of the world gits here."

Ro, bless him, looks like he might up and cry when I say this. But instead of lettin' tears fall, he lifts his head off his hands and reaches out, cups the outside of my hands with his own, touches my cheeks. "Everyone I called a friend is dead. But you? You're still here. You'll be alive when we fix this world, May. We'll put the dust to rest."

After that, I won't lie, things is real warm 'tween us. As the days pass and we go about our daily farm activities, I find it more and more difficult to keep my distance, despite my best efforts. And I don't avert my eyes when I spot him down by the well, sponge bathin' and naked from the waist up. The red pendant he wears, a symbol of his lucky status in society, gleams in the light like it's his lifeforce. It rests against his chest, lean muscles tense and firm from desert travel and farm labor. That handsome Ro, he thinks I'm a gift from the desert, but I know different. He's the desert's ransom, sent to me in exchange fer the land and people it took.

He asks if I'll show him how to use Frank, and I tell him that'd be wise cuz he ain't got no sense of how to use a firearm, and you never know when that kind of skill might come in handy out here. What I don't tell him is that the real reason I consent so quick is cuz it means I have an excuse to stand right up next to him, checking his aim and what not.

Fortunately fer my limited supply of ammo, that city boy learns purdy quick, but he still claims to need help with his stance. Apparently, my willingness to close the space between us during firearm training hasn't failed his notice.

Nine days after his arrival, I'm busy milkin' Reba, when he enters the paddock and kneels behind my stool, his body pressed up against me in a way that cain't be no accident. I cain feel all them muscles I saw by the pump just the day before, along with another one in particular that had still been hidden from view. He runs his fingers down my arms, grabs my hands, and kisses the back of my neck, just once. But just once is enough to send a shiver straight through me.

"Tell me to move away and I will." His lips brush my neck as he speaks. I don't tell him to move. In fact, I don't say nothing. "May, I know I don't deserve you, but that doesn't stop me from wanting you."

He kisses my neck again. "I can hardly bear it," he breathes.

He ain't the only one who's havin' trouble with composure. I turn myself toward him, rest my head against his shoulder, let him circle his arms 'round me.

"Yer leg's healin.' That mean yer fixin' to leave soon?"

He brings his arms down and scoots back a bit. I hate that I'm 'bout to ruin the moment but some things gotta be straightened out 'fore this sort of activity cain continue. I ain't shootin' tin cans with him and Frank no more—we're way beyond brushin' shoulders and correcting stances.

"I'm just wonderin', Rordan. You wanna bed me 'fore you head out into the dust, never to see me again? Is that yer aim?"

Ro stands up, the offended look I know too well plastered on him, and he walks clear out of the paddock without no kind of smart retort. Just walks away; part of me thinks he'll keep on walkin' straight out

into the desert and beyond. This is it, then. I turn back to the milkin',
tears streamin' out of my eyes at twice the pace as the milk flows from
Reba.

Why'd he have to show up here? Why'd he have to make me feel like
I'm both a gift and gifted? I should've known better. This is a place
that takes and takes and takes. It don't give nothin' without a blood
sacrifice.

I've been a fool. Granddad's dead or gone, and that's what Ro will
be too; gone and most likely dead soon as the desert decides it's done
with him. There ain't nothin' but our own lone selves on this planet.
It ain't a place fer buildin' attachments.

After my chores and a look 'round the farm, tryin' to suss out where
Ro got to, which is nowhere as I cain tell, I go inside and spend the heat
of the day sprawled over my bed, thinkin' 'bout the feel of his lips on
my neck, and his eyes that match the cloudless sky. He ain't left, not
really and truly left, cuz his bag is still here with his booklets, and ain't
no way he'd abandon those just cuz he and I had a tiff. But if that's so,
where's he got himself to?

The afternoon draws on and I'm worried now. I sit out on the
porch, Frank restin' in his favorite spot against the post. Maybe he took
a walk in the gulch and stumbled off a ledge. Maybe he headed north
but the law passed by and he got himself apprehended. Maybe, maybe,
maybe. The maybes don't come up with nothin' good.

I'm 'bout to give up hope when there he is, come 'round the side of
the house, surprisin' me with the suddenness of his arrival. He looks
like he's 'bout to get huffy with me again, but at that point, the thing
that seems most logical fer me to do is to burst into tears.

"I thought you'd gone." I wipe at my eyes. I don't know if I'm cryin'
cuz I'm happy he's here or cuz I'm mad at myself fer carin' so much
that he is. I do know that what I told him is true. Yeah, he left his bag,

I know, but the maybes still convinced me he wasn't comin' back. "I truly thought you'd gone."

All his anger blows out of him and he rushes to me, picks me up in his arms and keeps me there. "I'm here... I'm here now."

I don't know what to say so I just hold on to him tighter. Finally, he sets me back on my feet. "I've got a surprise for you, May."

He takes my hand and leads me to the back of the house. Says he spent the day in the dead walnut grove located across the dead fields. Dead, dead, dead. Only, not quite. There's more life there than I realized, cuz he's gone and killed one of that grove's last remainin' inhabitants. There it lays, a big grey squirrel, all butchered and ready fer cookin'.

"Wilderness expeditions teach you to do that?" He nods, grinnin'. Purdy soon that grins gone and spread itself like the desert onto my own tear-stained face. "Well, here's to yer fake survival lessons then. Let's have ourselves a feast."

Ch. 5: In Place of the Gods

Havin' meat fryin' in the pan is a cause fer celebration if ever there was one. I send Ro out to give the girls a bit of extra grain cuz why not let 'em celebrate too. After that, he's gonna head back to that grove of dried up walnut trees. Says he's certain he spied a few nuts, and if they are there, then I may be a fool fer overlookin' that grove, but I still want them nuts.

While he's gone I set the squirrel to cookin' and then go into my parents' old room, the one I never sleep in even though their bed's five times more comfortable than the measly cot I use. In my ma's wardrobe, there's a flannel shirt with holes where the moths got at it, a tattered old skirt she used to wear on laundry day, and a sky blue dress, light and airy and perfect fer a summer evenin'. That's the one I'm lookin' fer. Right 'fore I put it on, I think maybe it won't fit cuz I'm not as broad-shouldered as my ma, but it's nearly perfect, shaped and gathered in just the right places. I twirl 'round in front of the cloudy mirror hanging on the back of the wardrobe's door, the dress fannin' out 'fore returnin' to its place, its hem ridin' just above my knees. Since my ma's dead, she won't mind me pilferin' from her meager stash of feminine items, so I take one more thing, a silver hair clip, and sweep as many of my curls back into it as I cain manage.

"There," I say to myself. I am my mother on her weddin' day, same dress, same hair clip, same dark curls. I just pray I have her same spirit too, that I cain get through my life without regrettin' that I have to get through it at all.

I go back and tend to supper and 'fore long, Ro is poundin' up the steps. I got just enough time to reach back and grip ma's silver clip, makin' sure it's still in place, when Ro bounds over the threshold.

"Someone's coming," he yell-whispers, and all thoughts of curled hair held back and bare legs under a dress the same color as his eyes falls away.

I rush over to the tiny window next to the front door. He's still a ways off, trudgin' down from the north. From town. But ain't no mistakin' him. He's carryin' his ridiculous family flag, wavin' red and yellow, like all town leaders do in these parts in order to announce themselves ahead of time, make sure folks cain make ready with the royal treatment 'fore they reach their front gate.

"That'd be Orin Longbow." An overwhelming urge to kick something floods through me. "Ain't good."

"Why... why isn't it good?" Ro is all nerves, which frankly, is how he should be.

"Cuz Orin, aside from bein' a son-of-a-bitch, and I mean that quite literally, is also the town leader's son." Orin Longbow. He would love one of them rolls in the hay all the young men show up hopin' to git. Thing about Orin is, he's about as despicable as he is plum stupid. Last I heard from him, he was tryin' to sweet talk me by comparin' my beauty to that of the women him and his father keep doped up at the tavern. Well, if that sort of flattery works on the town girls Orin normally chases after, I suppose it's cuz dumb attracts dumb. As it stands, I've declined his advances more times than I cain count.

"Git," I say to Ro. It won't do to have Orin find a strange man in my house. If word gits back to his father, Ro'll be in fer a world of trouble, and me with him.

Ro don't wanna go, but I don't got time fer his debatin'.

"You git now, Rordan. You want the lawfolk knowin' yer here? Cuz Orin's pa'll tell 'em right quick. Besides, I cain handle Orin."

Ro scans me up and down. I know he's takin' in my get-up fer the first time. "May, what is he coming here for. What does he want from you?"

Well I surely picked the wrong night to dress up purdy, but I don't tell this to Ro. "Git now, Rordan, or I'll revoke your house privileges. Go down to the shed and throw some hay on top of you. And do it now, 'fore he gits any closer."

Ro looks me over one more time, his frown fiercely set, and then he does what I say. I go back to cookin', pretendin' that this is just another night fer me and my lonesome. I git to thinkin' that some good might even come out of Orin's surprise visit. If I want an answer about what happened to Granddad, Orin may be just the one to give it.

It don't take long 'fore Orin's knockin' on the door.

"May June? You in there?"

You know I am, stupid, you cain see me through the window. Ain't nothin' I cain do to stop my eyes from rollin', but I put a smile on over my annoyance and open the door fer him.

"Why, Orin Longbow, to what do I owe the pleasure." I situate myself right on the threshold, the door cracked open only as much as it needs to be in the hope that he will take the hint and not try to come inside. Orin ain't much at figurin' out hints, though, and he's pushed his way past me 'fore the word 'pleasure' has a chance to pass my lips.

"May June." He tips his hat, and sits himself down in Granddad's rocker. "Something smells fine. You kill yourself another one of yer goats?"

I don't need to respond to that. Besides, if it's small talk Orin wants, he ain't bound to git it out of me. "What you here fer Orin? I was just 'bout to settle in fer the night."

Orin sets his left ankle onto his right knee and pushes off a bit, slowly rockin' himself, and lookin' about as content as a cat who's just caught himself a mouse. "Here I thought you'd be pleased to see me, a young woman out on this solitary farm, all alone. You is all alone, ain't you?"

"You know I am, Orin. Ain't that why yer here? You got news of my Granddad?"

"Ain't seen him since a week 'fore you come to town lookin' fer him."

My heart sinks a little. I had a hope, a tiny one maybe, but still a hope that he knew where Granddad got himself to.

Orin sniffs. "I've been walkin' all day from town just to git to you. Cuz like I said, I thought you might be lonely. You gonna give me something in exchange fer my thoughtfulness, May June?"

I don't like the way he's takin' in Ma's dress, so different from how Ro looked at me just a few minutes ago. He's a mean ol' cat with sharp claws, that Orin.

"Orin, I'm more likely to believe Reba and Nessie learned to talk than that you came to visit out of thoughtfulness. Thinkin' after people's welfare ain't one of yer more renowned attributes."

"Now yer just bein' downright mean, girl." He's got danger in him, and he expects me to shake and shiver till he finally pounces. But I won't. I'm sayin' all the wrong things, maybe, but I ain't no mouse. I cain't stop myself from sayin' them, whether they spark the danger in him or not.

"I want you out of here, Orin Longbow. You ain't welcome. I don't care who yer pa is."

Orin gits up, but he don't move toward the door the way I'd hoped he would. Instead he starts glancin' 'round the house like he's expectin' to find something. Or someone. My mind fills with dread.

"Speakin' of my father." His eyes scan the room. "Pa got a courier bird in from the officer's camp. Turns out they're lookin' fer someone, a criminal. Think he's somewhere in these parts."

"You don't say."

"Yup, it's true." Orin walks into Ma's and Pa's room, sweeps his hand under the bed, comin' away with nothin' but dust. "It's real excitin' to hunt down a fugitive of the law. That's what I've been helpin' Pa do. And fer yer information, since you was so interested in knowin' the reason I came here, that's why. Seems like he might've passed this way. You seen anyone out of place, May June?"

"Only you, standin' in my house, which is a place you are out of, soon as you'll remove yerself."

Orin whips 'round, comes back to where I'm leanin' on the table, the one I just remembered is set fer a party of two. He glances down at it. "You expectin' someone?"

I try to laugh it off. "Only you of course. I saw that flag of yers comin' from the window. I planned on havin' you fer dinner all along. I'm just givin' you a hard time."

He don't ease up when I say this. Instead his eyes narrow. He's close now, so close. Crooked grin, teeth coated with chewin' tar, grindin' together. Wide hips pressin' in. He don't leave me no breathin' room.

"I cain't believe we've been havin' sich a nice conversation." He pauses, puts his hands on my shoulders, holds them there real tight. "And all this time, you've been hidin' an illegal."

"I don't know what yer goin' on about." I try unsuccessfully to wriggle out of his hold.

"No?" He's wearin' the foulest smile you cain imagine. "This is too good, May June. Wait till Pa finds out. Course, if you and I came to an arrangement instead..."

"What kind of arrangement?" I ask, though of course I know exactly how he wants me arranged. Is he really willin' to trade my favors fer Ro's freedom?

"Yer a smart girl." Smile, smile, smile. "You don't want to end up in jail, do you?"

He pushes on me, guidin' me towards the back of the house.

"Orin, you gotta know, I hate you. No matter what, I hate you."

Orin squints his eyes again. "Maybe I'll just report that illegal firearm to my pa after all."

Firearm? Cain he have been talkin' about Frank all this time? Frank, which some dumb ass farm girl left restin' plum out in the open in the corner next to the fireplace. Well if he thinks I'm goin' to invite him into my bed on account of Frank, he's got another thing comin'. Sorry Frank, but you ain't no flesh and bones and blue-eyed man, and there's a limit as to what I'm goin' to do fer yer sake.

"Now see here, Orin, I ain't agreein' to no arrangement with you. Take the gun if you have to. I'm sure yer pa won't mind addin' it to his collection. But leave me alone."

Orin's not gonna do that, though, that's fer damn sure. Those tobacco teeth and that glint in his eye tell me exactly what he ain't gonna let alone. "I come all this way May June, to check up on you."

"And now you have, so you cain leave."

"You know, you was always a stuck up one, never turnin' yer head when you passed me. And so proud of yer Granddad, you couldn't see him fer what he was, nothin' but a drunk."

"You don't talk about him, Orin. Besides, yer one to talk when it comes to limitin' yer liquor consumption."

He don't even acknowledge this, just keeps on blabberin'.

"But if there's one thing I cain say fer the old man, it's that he kept you after yer folks up and died. Kept you in line, too." Orin insists upon walkin' me backwards, so I both know and don't know what's comin' next. "But where's he now, May June? He ain't here to mind you no more, is he? Seems you need another man to teach you what's what."

"I don't need no man," I spit at him.

"No?" he sneers. "What about the one yer hidin' here. If you don't need him, then I best take him back to my Pa."

Shit, he knows. He knows about Ro. He was just playin' with me this whole time, just bidin' his time till he could pounce.

"You cain't do this, Orin."

But he cain. He knows he cain. He's hungry now. Got no more time to let his prey pretend she cain still git free.

"I bet he's hidin' outside somewhere." He licks his lips. "Ain't he?"

I don't say nothin'.

"Answer me."

"There ain't no one here but you and me. I told you that, Orin."

He takes his hands off of my shoulders, but there ain't no place I cain escape to now.

"Will he care what I do to you, May June? Will he come runnin' if he hears you beggin' me to stop?"

His tar mouth comes down over mine, but I twist my head to the side. I cain't stand Orin Longbow, I cain't stand what's 'bout to happen. I cain't stand it so much that I scream, cuz it's the only thing left to do, even though I know it's what he wants.

I'm screamin' "No, Orin!" and then he's grabbin' me again, rougher this time, and I'm just screamin', no need fer words. His hands twist my wrists and he leans his weight into me till I cain't stay upright no more. I may be smarter than Orin, but I'm no match fer him in size or strength. Orin, whose pa could afford to feed him adequately all the years of his growin' up, is a force against the wind.

I stumble backward onto my sleeping cot, which is the exact last place I wanna find myself what with Orin here. Orin comes right down onto it with me, his breath like curdled milk and rank tobacco hot against my neck. He fits himself on me, knee pressed to my thigh real painful, and that's when my screams once again change up, into bites this time. I chomp down hard on the only piece of Orin I have access to—his ugly crooked nose.

Ain't no smile on his face no more.

That's when he decides he's had just about enough of me. I've made plenty of noise to draw out Ro, if that's what he wants, so now he'd prefer if I was silent. He takes his hand, forms it into a ball, and slams it into my face.

All that frantic scratchin', clawin', bitin', screamin', it dries up like the fields and the walnut grove and like the well will too one day. I got no voice now, no fight, cuz it's not so much the punch that does me, it's the fact that the force of the blow sends my head smack into the corner of the window sill runnin' along the length of my bed.

This opens me up to a new kind of experience, one in which I get to taste my own blood as it makes its way down into my mouth. I should by all rights be unconscious by now. One eye refuses to open, and the other blinks thick and red, but the sight and awareness I got left in me is enough to grasp the followin'— Frank raised up and aimed high.

Frank, tried and true companion to one May June Stebbins — so help me if Orin uses him to do me in, I don't know what. Well, I must've got hit hard enough to knock the sense clear out of me. Cuz it ain't Orin who's got Frank in hand, it's Ro. I don't think Orin fully thought out what he was doin' when he aimed to draw Ro to him. And now, he's so busy with me, he don't even notice Ro is here.

Orin's pushin' Ma's pretty blue dress, all torn and bloodied now, up 'round my waist when Ro hauls him off me and uses Frank's backside to smack him to the floor. I blink away more blood and try to raise myself up a few inches, cuz I surely do not wanna miss this.

Orin's down on his knees, but he ain't about to admit defeat. He pushes against Ro's middle knockin' him off balance. This is the opportunity Orin needs to grab fer Frank. Frank's not havin' it and neither is Ro, but still, Orin puts up a good fight. Both men have their hands on Frank, and at first, Frank has the decency to stay aimed at the ceiling. Then Orin uses those big meat-fer-dinner-every-day muscles of his to turn Frank in the direction I was hopin' could be avoided. I shrink back on the bed as Orin struggles to aim Frank so he cain put a bullet right 'tween the two wounds he's already inflicted on me. Third time's a charm.

Don't do it, Frank, I think. And he won't do it. Ro won't let him. This is Orin's fatal mistake, really, cuz Ro's eyes blaze when he realizes Orin intends me to be the recipient of Frank's bullet.

Ro uses all his strength. All. Of. It. He turns Frank back in a direction far more in keepin' with Frank's disposition, back on the one who started this whole mess in the first place.

It comes like a new year's celebration, a blast of white and red to light up the night. And then I'm screamin' again, screamin' and I don't know if it's words, or bites, or just plain noise comin' out of me, but

I don't stop. I don't stop, not till Ro's own cries of "gods, gods, gods," over and over again turns into "May, May, May."

Quiet follows. I shut my one good eye, cuz there's gore splattered all over Ro and I cain't bear to see it. He lifts me into his arms, presses me into the blood he spilt fer my sake. I'm so tired, and the room's spinnin' faster and faster, and I don't wanna be here in this spinnin' fallin' down house, nor on this nearly dead farm, with its yield of nothin' but hardship and pain. I got only a few words fer Ro and then there ain't nothin' left fer me to give.

"Cain I go now?"

Red in my eyes, followed by blindness, my world's closing up fast. But my ears, ringin' from the shotgun blast, hold out long enough to make out the words, "No, May, you can't go. You can't go. May, don't go. May? May!"

He's shakin' me, callin' out my name in place of the gods, but I don't respond, cuz I'm already gone.

Ch. 6: The Life of the Dead and Dying

I guess that ain't the end of me, or this story would be a lot shorter.

When I come back, and that takes a mighty long time, Ro has cleaned up real good. I don't know where he put Orin, but the pieces of Orin that didn't stay attached to the rest of him are all wiped clear away, includin' the parts that Frank deposited all over Ro. Ro is right beside me, watchin' me with his clear blue eyes, like he knew I would choose this precise moment to open mine.

Judging from the sun, it's already midday. I've done slept a good fifteen hours. It takes me a second to realize more than just the time of day has changed. Ro must have found Granddad's raiser, cuz his scruffs all gone.

"You look different," I say and then think, I must surely too. My punched-in eye's still swollen shut most the way, and I must look a sight. I reach toward the bandage restin' on my right temple, but Ro's hand gits there first. He brushes it along my face, then grabs onto my fingers and presses them to his chest.

"I can't do this, May."

"Do what?" I try to sit up a bit, but it ain't easy.

"I can't." He squeezes my hand and lets go of it. "I can't leave here and be thinking of you all the time, wondering when the next asshole's going to come along and start an argument with you and Frank, or what's going to come of you when those goats stop producing. I can't do this, May. I've got my own problems. I can't care about you."

Well, that done set my kettle to boil, cuz I'm the one who took him in, fed him, sort of, and no worries about what regulations he might have broken or what crooked lawfolk he might lead my way, and I'm his problem? At the same time, he mentioned that he cain't care about me, which is basically a confession that he does care, so I keep my anger in check by usin' my words, use yer words, May, rather than my hand slapped right across his cheek.

"Fer yer information, I was gettin' by 'fore you came along and I'll do the same on my own after you leave. Till Granddad gits back, that is. Next up, I don't remember holdin' a sign out at the edge of the gulch beggin' fer lawbreakers to take up residence in my goat shed just in case trouble comes my way. And finally, as fer men comin' to harass me, Orin would never have come up here if it wasn't fer the fact that he was lookin' fer you!"

I force myself to sit up as best I cain, even though it makes the world take on a sideways sort of nature that feels most disconcertin'. "So if this is a contest about whose problems are givin' the other one the most grief, I say me and this beat-in head of mine win, hands down."

This shuts him up right quick. It's my turn to have me a starin' contest with mister blue eyes, and all bets should be on me as the winner, but he don't let go and he don't let go, and he brings his hand back up to my face, strokin' me where Orin did his damage. "This is my fault. Gods, May. I should have left after that first morning, bad leg or not."

"He still would've come lookin' fer you, lookin' fer trouble too, and you wouldn't have been here to prevent him from causin' some. He would've done a whole lot worse to me if you hadn't stopped him, and you know it."

His hand ceases it's back and forth movement across my brow, and he leans his forehead down till it brushes against mine. Only then do we call a draw to our starin' contest, it no longer bein' necessary.

"I'm sorry. I'm so sorry May. I've brought this to your doorstep, but I promise, I'll make it right."

And how you goin' to do that, huh Ro? That's what I wanna ask him. Kill all the lawfolk who come out lookin' fer you? Kill Orin's pa, cuz you know he'll be askin' after his son sooner rather than later. While yer at it, maybe you could find my Granddad, haul his ass back here, and then stop the dust from wakin', bring the cough to its knees, and make it rain, fill our bellies with nature's bounty. That would make it right.

That would make everything right.

Well, it ain't fair to lay all that on him, or maybe it is, but I'm feelin' charitable, so instead, I take in the scent of him, sage and goat milk soap, and then I ask, "Where should we bury the body?"

The dead and dyin' walnut grove just got itself a new citizen. Ro does a good job disposin' of Orin's remains, buried deep and wrapped in that gaudy flag of his. Ro thought the grove would work out real good on account of the fact that there's still roots there to hold the soil together. Cuz all we need is to do the work of buryin' a body, just to have the next strong wind come along and undo that work, exposin' our sins to the world once more. No, this way, our sins is bound to stay buried.

I set my head against the scratchy bark of a particularly tall tree—the only headstone Orin Longbow is ever gonna git. I'm tryin' to feel bad fer his fate and our hand in it. But I cain't. Orin made his choice to attack me, and the only reason he got shot to pieces is cuz he couldn't stand to lose what he thought was his. I ain't sorry to see him gone, but I do feel bad that Ro had to be involved. He killed a man. He did it to defend me, and the world's a lighter shade of grey cuz Orin ain't here no more, but still. It ain't the act of killin' so much as acceptin' fully that you done what you had to do.

"Rordan, you all right with this? I mean, with what happened. I'm awful sorry it came down to his demise, and you bein' the one to do the job. You know that don't you?"

Ro leans against the shovel that done just finished buryin' Orin and he sighs real deep. "Am I a bad person for not feeling worse about this, May?" He walks over, stands near me in sich a way that my heart takes to flutterin'. He sets his head against the tree just as I have mine, so that our faces are right next to each other.

"Every day, I think about my friends who died in the press fire. I think about Stuart, who suffered dearly for his betrayal. I picture each one in my head and I go over everything, wondering what I could have done to prevent all of that from happening." He pauses fer a moment, then nods his head slightly, like he's finally decided on something.

"When I think about Orin, though, what I picture in my head is you. You, with Orin bashing in your head and coming nearer to killing you then I can..." He cain't quite finish that thought. Instead he breathes in and out real slow. "I think about what he was about to do to you, May, and more than anything, the expression on your face when he pointed the gun at your head, like you knew without a doubt that you were going to die. So no, I'm not all right with any of this, the deaths, the injustice, the lies, a world that would create men like Orin.

I'm not all right with it, but I'm glad I did what I did. And I would do it again, ten times over if it meant keeping you alive, May. Believe me when I say that."

Oh, I believe him all right, and it terrifies and thrills me all at once. Never did I imagine I'd meet a man who would kill fer me. This alone don't seem so odd, cuz I was willin' to do some pretty nasty things when I thought it would keep Ro safe. If he was in harm's way and I had the means to remove that harm, of course I'd do it. But what truly scares me is, where's this goin'? He cain't stay here, I know he don't wanna stay, but these sort of proclamations he's makin', that he'd keep me alive no matter what—it's like he already thought this out, thoughts about him and me that he ain't shared yet.

"I cain't be dependent upon you fer my survival. You know that, don't you? Yer gonna have to leave, and I honestly don't know what I'll do then, but I'll have to think of somcthing."

"May." He turns his head so his lips are right next to my ear. "Do you want me to go?"

"I cain't bear the thought of you leavin', Ro." That declaration earns me a smile, cuz I gave him the answer he was hopin' fer and finally said his name the way he likes, all in one sentence. "But you're a lawbreaker and the law's got wind that yer here. You cain't stay."

"Neither can you." He kisses my cheek, then runs his lips up to my ear, tugging on it with his teeth. I gasp at the sensation it stirs in me. His next words are a whisper of warm air across my skin. "Come with me May."

His lips trace a hot line across my jaw, and then they find my own. "Come with me." He kisses me long and deep, and finally, I taste him, the city life, the courage of his pursuits, the pain of betrayal, the miles of wilderness, of runnin', the desert alive and ravenous under his feet, the constant hunger and thirst and the will to keep goin', the lonely farm house with the curly-haired girl standin' on the porch. I taste it all in him. And I know, this ain't no roll in the hay fer him, not fer neither of us.

This is the moment when the facts and truths of our lives converge, when our stories become a tale we tell together. It's a certainty that he feels this too. He breaks away from me long enough to say, "If you won't come with me, I won't go without you. I'd rather stay and face the law then leave you behind. I need you, May. You're my only source of water in all the desert."

What he means is, he cain't live without me. I don't know how it's possible. We've only known each other fer what – goin' on two weeks or so -- and if he'd said it ten minutes ago, I'd have argued with him about how it cain't be that way 'tween us. Sich thinkin' cain only end in heartache, cain't it? But I don't argue with him now. How cain I dispute something I feel is true deep within my own heart as well? Maybe Ro was right all along about the dust. It has the power to stir itself and those it choses till we are truly and fully awake. I cain't never return to the state of unknowing I had been in, 'fore Ro crossed my path.

    #

We move up to the house then, cuz it ain't appropriate to do what we was doin' right next to Orin's freshly dug grave. Orin. Dead Orin. And now we're about to... what kind of people are we anyhow? But I suppose that's it, we're just people, two people who've been on their own fer far too long.

I don't got much time to dwell on Orin, or if I'm good or bad or something in between 'fore Ro takes all them thoughts from me. Then there's only him, him leadin' me upstairs to the loft, cuz I cain't do this in my parent's room, I just cain't. He kisses me and then holds me to him, sayin' "May, May, May," and he lets me go enough so that he cain tug at my coveralls, droppin' one strap and then the other over my shoulders so that they fall away from me all together. I raise my shirt up over my head and then I'm there, stark-naked and not one bit shy, cuz however I am, I am me. And I'd rather be exactly who I am, standin' here right now with Ro, then anyone else anywhere in this world or any other.

Maybe, I got some luck in me after all.

"I've never met anyone like you." He runs his fingers along my sides. I don't stop them fingers, wherever they wanna travel. He grabs my backside and presses me to him. "You're perfect."

"Ain't no sich thing." I tug on his belt, undoin' his fly. "But I think I will accept yer flattery none-the-less."

Ro breathes in and lets out a low moan as I relieve him of his drawers. "But you are, May. You're incredible."

I smile and with one hand at work where his drawers used to be, I use the other to bring his head back down to mine. "Incredible, huh? Well, yer about to find out just how right you are."

Ro's eyes, blue, blue, blue, loose their control at this point. He moans again and two seconds later, I'm lying on the bed, his ruby medallion danglin' over me, sending a spectrum of fiery light 'round the room. "I dreamed of this ever since the first night I came here." Every word is a tremblin'. He cups my breast and brings his tongue down to it, licking circles over the tender flesh. Oh gods, if I wasn't ready fer him by now, this is all it takes to get me there.

"Ro," I struggle to keep an iota of composure so my words come out logical. "I'll go with you, I'll go."

He brings his head up long enough fer his eyes to show me everything — happiness, lust, love, relief.

There ain't nothin' that cain stop us, not the lawfolk, nor the desert, not the cough. Nothin'. Ro knows what to do now, the dominion of the dust awake inside me, inside us. And ain't nothin' cain stop that power from spreadin' over every part of who we are.

Ch. 7: The Trials

R o thinks he knows how to git through the harsh stretch of desert awaitin' us, but the problem is, it's gonna take a little time to make his plan happen. If it works at all. We got several more days here on the farm, at least, and that means several days to fear Orin's pa and his law friends showin' up.

"Reba and Nessie weren't never trained to be pack animals." I try my best to impress this point upon Ro as he finishes hitchin' the girls up side by side. He's got a sled ready and waitin' fer 'em made in haste out of an old sheet of tin that used to cover the north side of the shed. "They're just milk goats."

Ro's plan is to git the girls to do the hard work of travelin' by carryin' some of our supplies on their backs and pullin' us fer at least part of the way. Them goats are scrappy, and they're stronger than they look. So it ain't a bad idea, 'cept when you think about how you gonna direct 'em and keep 'em movin' forward. Ain't they gonna resist that on account of it's a lot more work haulin' water and people over the dust than what they're used to doin'? And by "used to doin'" I mean standin' 'round in their pen or, if they're feelin' particularly ambitious, breakin' through the fence so they cain destroy my lettuces.

It may be futile, but I agree to let him try. I know his ankle still gives him grief, though he won't admit it. I think he's worried he'll slow me down out there, and the desert ain't no place fer takin' a leisurely stroll. We gotta go and go and go.

It's a good thing Ro's got them two goats wrapped 'round his finger. I don't know what it is 'bout him that calms them so, but they tolerate him tyin' ropes 'round them to create a sort of halter, a contraption they never wore before in their lives. 'Fore he attaches them to the sled, he takes the reigns and leads them 'round the yard. At first, they wanna stop every two seconds, whenever they spy something they think is edible, which fer a goat is purdy much everything. But he nudges them on and they comply. He awards them with a handful of our dwindlin' supply of grain, one of the many necessities Granddad failed to bring back from town all them months ago.

We take 'em through this same routine again that day, and three times the next. I do my share of guidin' 'em 'round, cuz if I don't make him, Ro won't rest that ankle nearly as much as he should. We go on like this fer a whole week, anxious every day that we've spent one day too long here. Finally, it's decided they gotta be ready fer the sled. Once he gits it attached, and that takes some doin' given the limit of our supplies and experience in sich matters, Ro hands the reigns over to me. "We should start them out slowly, build up to the full weight. You're lighter than me, May."

"Yeah, but they like you better." I imagine them goats flyin' every which way till they dump my ass in the dust. Still, I am curious as to how this is all gonna work out, so I set myself down on the sled and hold the reigns in my hand like I saw in one of them books about horses Pa gave me as a child. The girls don't go nowhere. "Now what?"

Ro looks thoughtful, which I take to mean that he ain't got no idea. After a moment, inspiration must alight inside him, though, cuz he sticks out his hand and gives Reba a little swat on her backside, then does the same to Nessie. "Go," he says. "Git."

"Did you just say 'git'?" Well I guess he chose his desert lingo correctly, cuz at that moment, I feel myself jerked back as the sled begins to move forward. "Oh my gods, Ro, it's workin'!"

I grab the edge of the sled to steady myself and try to keep hold of the reins as we thump along.

"Go," I say, "Git." I slap the reins against the girls, hopin' that it keeps 'em movin' without hurtin' 'em none. They stick with their forward momentum, even pickin' up speed a bit.

As we leave the yard and hit the used-to-be fields where the dust has nearly taken hold, the bumpin' and jostlin' lessen. It's gonna be a smooth sail over all them dunes out in the desert, I cain see it now. Ro jogs alongside the sled as best he cain, and I give him a big smile. I was right to trust him. There're some mighty fine notions in that head of his.

"Steer, May!" he yells at me.

"What?" I don't know what he means. I thought a steer was one of them animals from our ancestors' world—a male cow. These ain't no cows, though. The wind whips my hair across my face. I wish I had an extra hand to brush it away, but one hand holds the reins and the other's clenched tight to the sled and it's got no intention of lettin' go.

"Use the reigns to make them turn," he shouts over the wind. "Pull on the left and they'll go left. Pull on the right and they'll go right."

"Well, I'll try." I give the left hand ropes a tug, thems the ones that are on Nessie's side. Sure 'nuff, Nessie turns left, and Reba with her since they're tied together and she ain't got no choice in the matter. "Git," I cry.

I practice this several more times. Left, right, left, right, and then lead 'em back to their paddock. When we finally come to a halt, Ro takes the reins from me and pulls me up. I nearly fall back over, my body cain't quite believe it's in one place again. Ro catches me and brings me to him, laughin' all the while.

"You did it!" He spins me 'round.

"Yeah, not like you had a hand in it or nothin'." I kiss him quick and then we see to the girls, relievin' 'em of their burdens and givin' 'em more grain than we should on account of how joyful we are that we're on the cusp of an actual escape.

Tomorrow, we'll practice again, only this time, both of us will be loaded in the sled, plus all our gear. If they cain handle that, then by the day after tomorrow, we'll be on our way, ridin' the dust south, and hopin' that it tolerates our passage, goats and all.

\#

He ain't drunk. That's the first thing I notice, and that's how I come to know right from the beginnin' that this is a fantasy I'm havin' while fast asleep.

"Only in my dreams would you come back to the farm whole and sober." Granddad grins at my words and sets himself next to me on the porch. His eyes are clear and alert.

"This used to be a beautiful place," dream Granddad tells me. "Them fields were green. That was before you came along, Missy May."

Missy May. He ain't called me that since I was shorter than the fence running 'round the goat pen.

I git me an impatient sort of feelin'. I should be happy to see him, cuz he's finally back, but then again, this ain't but a dream. If he was here fer real, that'd be different. As it stands, I still got me some unanswered questions.

"You never came back. Why'd you leave me all alone here?" If I cain't accuse the real Granddad, this dream one will have to do.

His grin disappears and his eyes crinkle at the corners. "Some things cain't be helped, May."

I snort. "That ain't no explanation. It ain't even an excuse, much less an apology."

"Am I to blame, girl?" He shakes his head. "I cain't rightly say. I don't know what happened to me."

"Well, that makes two of us then, so we're right back where we started."

Granddad places his feet on the railing and tilts his chair back. "I ain't here to talk about me, anyways. It's you I need to see to."

Because he did such a swell job of it in the past, I suppose. I huff a bit, but I figure it cain't hurt none to hear him out. "What about me then, Granddad?"

He puts his feet back down on the ground and turns to me. "Yer in what they call 'quite a quandary.' And what that means is, you gotta go, May."

Just how much does this fake Granddad truly know about my predicament? "What's that now?"

"Missy May, you ain't got the time you think you have. This ain't yer home no more."

Ain't my home? "It's not like I got a summer lake house to vacation at. This farm's the only home I know."

Granddad turns his head from side to side. "Well, look at that, it ain't day no more."

In the span of that sentence, the light of the sun has slipped away, and, as though there needs to be something to replace it with, a mighty wind whips up something awful in its wake. Granddad's eyes hold a squall. They command the air's roilin' course as it churns 'round us. Boards held by rusty nails to the sides of the house start to come undone, slammin' against the house's frame. With a squeal, I throw myself to the floor, holdin' my arms over my head. Like that'll be enough to save me from—from whatever this is.

"This is." He says the words at the same time I think 'em. He's reading my mind now, which makes perfect sense to me in the dream. It's expected, in fact, cuz ain't he just a bunch of my thoughts and deliberations bunched together into Granddad form anyhow? I cain't ferget that this is my dream. I'm makin' all this occur.

"This is," he repeats, "where folks like me die, Missy May. Not you, though. I ain't intendin' it to be yer end, too."

"Stop this, Granddad! Stop it, or surely I will die!"

"You stop it," he shouts at me. "Yer the one. Damn it May, this is on you!" He is drunk now, old Granddad. Drunk on the wind and the dust it carries. "Pick yerself up and go!"

He grabs my shoulders, cold bony hands lift me from the floor. Soon as I'm standin' I send my feet flying. Off the porch, past the goat shed, out into the field filled with a starless darkness. I run with no sense in where I'm goin' and no vision to git me wherever I'm headed. Granddad's voice carries on the wind and he says I shouldn't stop so I don't. I let the wind transport me away from the home that ain't my home no more, until I burst from the darkness back into the day.

I'm surrounded by sand—real sand. The beach kind. But here, there ain't no water to accompany it as far as I cain see. My feet, suddenly without their customary boots, sink into the sand's warmth. Toes curl, diggin' themselves under shells broken down into fine grains by nonexistent waves.

I turn myself around, strainin' to peer over the dunes, and that's when he appears.

Ro.

He's standin' next to me where he wasn't just a second before, but at the same time, I git the feelin' he's been alongside me ever since the beginnin'. Since all that sand was the living shells of sea creatures and this barren stretch was a teaming tidal pool.

"My home is gone." He says it, but he don't look sad about it.

"Mine too." We've both been stripped bare of our past. We are both fleeing a home that no longer welcomes us.

The past is gone, but home — well, that's yet to be discovered. I'm filled with assurance. With purpose. Our true home is out there. It's waitin' fer us. Past the dust and the sand. Past whatever is beyond.

Together, we take a step forward.

Sun shines through the square window in Granddad's loft. It's the mornin' of our last full day at the farm. Our final goat-sled test day. I watch Ro sleepin', his fair head adrift in dreams, and I recall my own, or parts of it, anyways. I cain't deny the truth now—that I am meant to go out into the world with this man. Everything about being with him feels right. But there was more to that dream, wasn't there? I'm purdy sure Granddad made an appearance, but that part's hazy now. All I cain see is Ro walkin' next to me toward a blue horizon.

I got me a faint nigglin' that I should feel a sense of urgency, but I cain't seem to push that feelin' all the way to the surface. Instead, I finger Ro's glossy hair, then rub the golden stubble grown back on his chin. He smiles and them blue eyes open, givin' me the once over.

"Good morning." He traces the outline of my bare shoulder with his fingers.

I give him a good morning all right, a very good morning judgin' from his reactions, and when that's over I lie back down with my head buried in his chest.

"I never did tell you how pretty you looked in that blue dress, May." His voice is still sleepy, peaceful. "I'm sorry it got ruined."

"Ain't like I need it now." What good would it do me out there on the dust? But I must confess, I've packed Ma's silver hair clip to take with us. There're some things you just cain't leave behind.

A poundin' on the door sets us both bolt upright. Shit. That's the only word that comes to mind fer about five seconds. And then it hits me all at once—Granddad's warnin', the farm fallin' to pieces and me runnin' fer my life. Ain't it just like Granddad? Even in a dream, he shows up too late to do any good. Had he gotten himself into my brain one day earlier, we could have heeded his warnin' and been gone by now.

Well, there's no sense in dwellin' on all that. I gotta calm myself, keep from panickin'.

"Stay up here," I tell Ro while pullin' my coveralls on. "Hide yerself. Whoever it is, I'll git rid of 'em."

"May, wait." He pulls on my arm as I move to go down the ladder. The poundin' on the front door repeats itself.

"Whoever it is is gonna invite himself in soon, Ro. He ain't gonna go away simply cuz we don't respond." Ro sets his face to one of dissatisfaction, but he lets me go and hugs Frank to his chest instead.

I climb down from the loft, and head to the front door. When I open it, there stands Orin's pa, just like I suspected.

"Why, Mr. Longbow, hello there." I give him a big smile. "You must've read my mind about how lonesome I've been out here. How nice of you to pay a visit. You wanna come in?"

"Miss Stebbins." Jacob Longbow removes his hat and enters the house. "Don't mind if I do. Been walkin' all night to git here."

"And with that wind against you, too. Well now, you must be exhausted. Yer welcome to sleep in my folks' old room, case you're in need of a rest."

"I thank you kindly." He slumps into a seat at the table and adjusts his belt to compensate fer his repositioned girth. "I wish I had time fer sich luxuries as rest, but I'm afraid I've business with you of a pressin' matter."

"Is it my Granddad?" I cain't feel no dread at what his response might be. I only wanna know fer certain his life is over, so I cain get on with my own.

"No, Miss Stebbins, it's not yer Granddad, though I'm afraid his absence don't look too promisin'. I'm not sure in good conscience I cain let a young lady remain out here on her own. I told him as sich, on account of all the time he spent at my tavern that he'd have to tend to you better or else find you a husband. But he flat out refused." He raises an eyebrow like he really hopes I'm understandin' what he's sayin' and maybe what he's leavin' unsaid too. "I know you love yer Granddad, he's yer kin and that means something. But his obstinance in regards to yer welfare went against what I know is right, you see?"

I nod like I cain't see, in fact. Play it like I'm too dumb to know where this is goin'. Course, he's just lookin' out fer me, just like his son was, sich upstandin' gentlemen as they are. Did Granddad git in the way of those honorable intentions of his? It seems likely. I cain't believe I hadn't thought of this before, especially after Orin showed up and made his own intentions known.

"Anyways, prospects fer yer future is a conversation to have after I've discussed that pressin' matter with you first."

"Well, all right." It takes all the strength I cain muster not to burst into tears. I have my answer, just like I wanted. I know it even if it don't make no sense to feel such a certainty after months of nothing but uncertainty: Granddad's dead. No way would he leave me to deal with the likes of Jacob Longbow and his son all on my own. Granddad may have been a lot of no good things, but he loved me, in his way, and he hated the Longbows' unsettlin' interest in me. Jacob knows more about Granddad's last moments then he's lettin' on, but as much as I wanna, it'd be unwise to press the issue at this juncture.

"Seems we have a dangerous lawbreaker in our parts. You know anything about that?"

"A lawbreaker?" I hold my hand up to my heart fer effect. "Am I in danger out here all by my lonesome?"

"You might be, Miss Stebbins. You probably are in fact. You sure you ain't heard about this criminal?"

"How could I have? Yer the first person I've seen since I came to town lookin' fer Granddad."

"Well, that just makes what I've gotta discuss with you that much more difficult fer me. Cuz I sent my son Orin out this way to check on you over a week ago, and no one's heard from him since. But you say you ain't seen him, huh?"

"I think I'd remember that, sir." I cluck my tongue and shake my head. "I cain't believe this. Do you suppose Orin had a run-in with this lawbreaker yer talkin' about on the way out here?"

"Cain't say fer sure. That's the assumption we're goin' with, though. I sent word to the officer's camp and they agreed to come out this way to search the area. Should be here sometime later today. Thought I'd let you know, 'fore you get alarmed at the presence of all them strangers."

"I appreciate you thinkin' of me, especially in light of yer son's disappearance. I cain't even begin to imagine how tryin' this must be fer you." I place my hand on his arm and give it a pat. Jacob puts his other hand on mine and holds it there.

"You know, gettin' to the rest of our conversation, I gotta tell you Miss Stebbins, ain't no need fer you to stay on this dust-blown no-good farm forever. Not when there's opportunities in town fer a purdy girl sich as yerself." He gives me a tar-filled grin, just like his son's. I try to pull my hand back, but he holds it there.

"Oh yeah? What kind of opportunities?"

He leans in towards me. "I think you know, Miss Stebbins. Girl like you could make me some money and do well fer herself besides. You'd be taken real good care of. Now, I know Orin has a fancy fer you, and who cain blame him. Soon as he's found, I'm sure he'd be glad yer takin' up residence above the tavern. Him and me, 'tween the two of us, we could teach you real good how to be pleasin' to the menfolk." He licks his lips, takes in a real heavy breath, like he's picturin' just what kind of teachin' he's gonna give me.

"I'm not sure I'm the kind of girl yer lookin' fer, Mr. Longbow."

"Oh, come now Miss Stebbins. Yer young and poor and desperate. Yer exactly the kind of girl I'm lookin' fer."

I close my eyes and pray that Ro stays hidden up in that loft, cuz I cain just imagine him goin' all Frank on Jacob Longbow's ass after listenin' to him shoot his mouth at me. But I don't need no more messes to clean up, not with the lawfolk descendin' on my farm later today. What I need is fer Jacob Longbow to go away.

"Mr. Longbow, I promise you I will take yer offer into consideration. But right now, the goats need milkin' and I've gotta think about hostin' a group of hungry men in a few hours. Now, yer welcome to stay and rest here, like I said previous, but I really must attend to my chores."

"Of course." Finally, Jacob lets go. He must think he's got me right where he wants me. "I'd love to stay, but I need to meet them officers four miles north of here so we cain investigate the area 'round Simmons Crossing 'fore headin' back to yer place. Now, won't them lawfolk gawk when they catch sight of you, purdy girl. Might even want to think 'bout startin' yer job early. I cain set that up fer you, just keep that in mind. Make sure none of 'em git too rough."

"Like I said, I'll consider it." I walk him to the door. "I hope you find Orin, Mr. Longbow."

Jacob puts his hat back on and gits to the act of leavin' my property. "Don't you worry about that, Miss Stebbins. Me and eight lawfolk—I think we cain handle it. Bye now."

I wait till he crosses the yard, cuts through the used-to-be fields, and passes over the horizon 'fore shuttin' myself back inside. Eight lawfolk. Eight! They must want Ro in shackles real bad fer what he done. I lean against the door, and here comes Ro down from his hidin' spot. He clings to me, breathes in the scent of my hair.

"You don't know how close I was to leaning Frank over the railing and blowing his head apart. The things he said to you...."

I kiss him and gently push him away. "You showed real restraint. But now we gotta pick up and go. If we hurry, we cain git out of here 'fore we ever gotta deal with that man again."

There won't be no more test runs. It's now or never. Just like in my dream, there ain't no time to say goodbye to the only home I've ever known. And Granddad? He's dead, I'm sure of it, but as to who's responsible, I'll never have that answered neither, though I will always suspect Jacob Longbow had a hand in it.

Much as I might like to, this ain't no occasion to wallow. We make our preparations, harvest everything from the garden that we cain, harness the girls, and hope the desert will protect us, cuz surely, there ain't no one else who will.

Ch. 8: Up the Rabbit Hole

It's too dang windy. I know I should be glad fer it cuz it means we're movin' at a fair speed. But when we stop to rest the goats, the wind don't stop with us.

We're maybe five or six miles south of the farm. The girls have been real toleratin' of us, but I don't know where their limit is at. We ain't seen sign of no one, and that's good, at least. Ro don't wanna stop, but I say we have to. It's the heat of the day and we all feel it something awful. We cain't push the girls through it like this. If the dust takes 'em, what do we do then?

We find some fallen trees, their wood long dried up, that act as a bit of cover, a break from the wind. Our backs to the largest one's twisted trunk, we hunker down, each of us havin' ourselves a carrot, Reba and Nessie included.

The heat passes, but the wind don't.

"Ain't good," I say as we git the girls harnessed again.

Ro holds his hand out to gage the wind, and his opinion don't deviate from mine. "Ain't good."

By evening, it feels like we're gettin' battered by bits and pieces of everything' that ever died out here in this desert. The goin' is slow, but still, we've put nearly fifteen miles 'tween us and the farm. Late that night we find us a dune to block out some of the wind, and we wrap up, the four of us, in our wool blankets. In the morning, ain't nothin' changed, but I know it's bound to soon. And a dune ain't gonna protect us when the time comes.

"This is just what you call the prelude," I tell Ro. "We need to find us some shelter, 'fore the storm hits." And by storm, I don't mean no thunder and rain, as you cain imagine.

We continue on, the girls bleatin' their disapproval. Ain't a goat in the world don't get antsy when they know a dust storm's on the horizon. Pretty soon, we gotta get up and walk, coaxin' them forward, always with an eye toward findin' us a place that'll save us from bein' buried alive.

"Come on Reba." I'm to the point of yellin' now, pullin' on her halter fer all it's worth. I hold out a few kernels of grain and she edges forward. They sky's grown dark, hours 'fore the sun's due to set.

"May." Ro's voice barely reaches me even though we ain't more than a few paces apart. "Up ahead."

There's a building, thank the gods. We finally convince the goats to make fer it, then come to find it ain't no more than an abandoned shack. But it'll do. Ro scrapes away the dust piled up at the foot of the door and then pries it open. It's just an empty room, stripped bare of all its contents long ago. I light our lantern and we get to haulin' in our stuff.

"Look fer cracks." I yank clothes and blankets out of our pack and hand them to Ro. "Anywheres the dirt cain make its way in—we gotta stop it."

We set to work, stuffin' bits of fabric 'round the door frame, 'tween loose slats of wood, into the joints separatin' the ceiling from the walls. When we finish, I stand there with this horrible notion, like we just lined our own coffin. The girls bleat nervously in the corner and I slide to the floor, lettin' Ro fold me in his arms.

"It'll pass tonight, most likely." I nestle in against him. "If this ramshackle hovel don't collapse on top of us, we'll be all right."

Ro glances 'round, calculatin' how far the walls already lean to the left. "I feel so reassured."

The building shakes and howls, and so do we. Goat bleats of terror, tremblin' farm girl wrapped up in her lawbreaker's embrace. We spend a fitful night. I try to stay awake, cuz ain't no way I wanna miss the last hours of my life if that's what these are. 'Fore long though, I cain't help myself, and off I go, into a sorta half sleep state where dreams flow from me, pretendin' they're as real as the sun searin' itself into our parched land.

I come to a crossroads, take the turn to the right and walk and walk and walk through the clay baked terrain. A man's up ahead. It's not Granddad this time, and I git a thrill at the thought that it's Ro, my Ro. But when I approach him, all happiness and light, it ain't Ro, it's Orin. Reba's slung over his shoulder, slaughtered, gutted, bloody, and he says, "I did you a favor May June. Killed you a goat. Now what you gonna give me fer the killin'? I think I deserve something mighty fine, don't you?"

Then he's on me, and the earth is shakin' under us, and the wind is howlin', howlin', howlin', and I try to push him off, but my hands come away from him all blood-stained, and I look where his face should be, at the bits and pieces of skin and bone and brain oozin' out of his head like cream of chicken soup bubblin' over the edge of a kettle, and I scream.

I cain't be sure my shriekin' makes any impression over the violence of the wind, not until Ro tightens his hold and says my name. "Come back." He calls me out of my dream, and what else cain I do but listen.

Cuz what's the use of wastin' terror on a dream nightmare when we've got a real one to fear.

The morning, or what I think's the morning, brings silence. But ain't no light to accompany it. Course, I say to myself, we done a good job of pluggin' the shack up fer holes. No way the sun cain git in.

Ro pulls his rolled up blanket away from the bottom of the door, where the biggest gap to the outside world is. Dust sifts in. We start unpluggin' everything', comin' away with nothin' but darkness and grit.

Ro shakes his head. Ain't good.

The world's had itself a renovation durin' the night. The desert put its mind towards redecoratin', and evidently, it saw this little shack as an affront to its ascetics.

We're goin' to have to dig ourselves out. But we don't know how much of dust got deposited on top of us. Maybe it's only a few inches. Maybe it's the whole dang desert.

After some debatin', we decide to pry loose several of the boards near the top of the shack on the side that's leanin' the worst. The wind was from the opposite direction, so we're hopin' there's less dust build up on that side. 'Fore we git started, we tie kerchiefs 'round our faces to keep the dust out as far as that's possible. I even manage to cover Reba and Nessie's muzzles, despite their protests. Ro uses his knife and sets to work diggin' out rusty nails, tearin' the boards from their place on the wall. Dust files in, and we jump out of its way. It settles to the bottom of the shack and then keeps comin', till the room's half air, half drift. Ain't no sunlight yet.

Ro and I look at each other. If our efforts don't create a rabbit hole to the surface 'fore the shack fills up with dust, we're done fer. Once the pile reaches up to the hole Ro made, it stops its flow, so we scoop and scoop away from the hole. The desert keeps invitin' itself in.

Purdy soon, we're standin' in dust up to our knees, and I have to help the girls git themselves on top of it. Won't be long now till there ain't no place fer us to climb to.

"You still think the dust's on yer side, Ro?" My fear and frustration's makin' me spiteful. But Ro, he ain't givin' up just yet.

He digs some more, and there's a desperation to him, same as there was the day he showed up at the farm, dehydrated and hopin' very much not to die.

"Come on!" He digs furiously. I do my best to keep the goats and all our stuff from bein' buried and try not to think about how much air we got left. He scoops and scoops, and I don't want 'em to be, but my eyes are damp, cuz we escaped Orin's Pa and all them lawfolk just to be drowned by the Dust. It ain't fair.

That's when the wall gives a sound like it's birthin' a baby, a kind of low, determined wail. I know as certain as the desert is dry that we ain't got much time till the roof collapses. We gotta be out of here 'fore that happens.

Ro is frantic now. He's got himself half into the hole and I cain picture it cavin' in on him, his feet flailin' till the suffocation stills him ferever. I pull on the goats' reins with one hand and scoop dust with the other. Anything to speed this along.

That's when it comes. The light. Faint at first, cuz Ro is all up in that hole now blockin' my view. But he hollers back to me and I know I ain't hallucinatin'. Ro struck air.

When he hops back into the shack, it's my turn to holler. 'What you doin' back in here? You got yerself out. You should've stayed out. This place is gonna be flat and gone any minute.

"That's why I'm back. You go first, May."

"Why? Cuz you need to feel like yer rescuin' me?"

Ro makes a doleful face. "May, we don't have time for this, just go!"

"Fine." I reach up to the hole and Ro grabs me 'round the waist and hoists me into it. The shack has another contraction. Wood stretches and heaves.

"Climb, May!"

"What you think I'm tryin' to do, plant a rose garden?" My hands grasp at loose dust. They slide down as I try to aim myself up. I make slow progress, but I keep my eye on the prize, a circle of blue above me.

Coughin' and wheezin', I break free onto the surface, the sun stingin' my eyes nearly shut. My weary muscles complain as I use them to crawl full out of that hole. I've got one of the harnesses attached to my waste. I throw it back down the hole, and soon there's a sharp tug. Not long after, our packs, our reserves of water, all our stuff, is up on the surface. I pass the rope back down again and this time, up comes a very perturbed goat.

"Nessie, it's good to see ya, girl."

"May?" Ro's voice is all hollow, like it's comin' from the other end of a mile-long tunnel.

"Here's the rope again." I toss it down.

"Reba's fighting me on this, May," Ro's tunnel voice reports.

Dang it, I cain't have that goat holdin' up this rescue operation.

"Tie her to the rope and leave her then. Git yer ass up here, Ro. We'll hoist her up after that."

Ro makes his way through the rabbit hole, but the shack ain't ready to birth this one. It gives a shudder; the ground beneath me begin to give.

"Hurry it up Ro. Use the rope!" I pull on my end of it, hopin' that'll help. Just a little more time. That's all we need.

But we don't git it.

I cain just make out the top of his fair head, coated with filth, as he edges toward the surface. That's when the shack gives way, and the hole with it. Grimy golden hair disappears, a grain of sand being sucked through an hour glass.

He's gone, and all my hope's gone with him.

Ch. 9: Our Daily Salvation

"**R**o! Oh gods." I pull on the rope but it don't give. Not. At. All.

I'm gonna lose him. Ro will be dead, and where will that leave me? Alone with a dang goat out in the middle of this godsdamn good fer nothing wasteland.

I keep tuggin' away, useless though my efforts may be, cuz what else am I supposed to do? I cain't give up. I don't give up even with that hopelessness pricklin' the back of my neck like it's a plague of lice come to suck me till I'm all hollowed out; nothing more than a blade of dried prairie grass.

Purdy soon though, I'm sittin' back instead, rope still taut in my hands, watchin' what I'd begun to think was impossible: as the shack gives itself to the desert, the dust has to relocate itself somewhere. It drains away, and slowly, the shiftin' ground releases him, lets him claw his way out the rabbit hole into the world again. I'm so shocked at Ro's resurrection, I cain barely move.

The desert, a place that takes and takes and takes—it gives, finally. It gives me back my Ro.

After I git over myself, I realized I cain't be still no more. The disbelief is gone and now I gotta act. I scoop dust away from him, which ain't easy seeing as though it's makin' a funnel, aimin' to suck him back down into the shack. But soon the shack is full up and that's when things git easier.

A little more strugglin' and he's free. I reach fer him, heave him onto my lap, clearin' away the dust from his eyes and nose and mouth as best I cain, barely thinkin' of poor Reba, lost to us fer sure, I am that relieved to have him back.

I didn't believe him about the desert handin' out favors, but now I get to thinkin' I was too quick to judge. Cuz here he is, sputterin' and breathin' hard, but breathin'. Alive. My Ro. And besides that, we got two days and a dust storm 'tween us and them lawfolk. Truth is, that storm almost killed the lot of us, but it may have saved us, too. If they was on our trail, Jacob Longbow and his lawfolk friends may not have even survived that storm, and now even if they did, there ain't no trail fer 'em to follow. The dust saw to that. Them men gonna be hard-pressed to find us now, and I cain't believe what I got to thank fer that.

Maybe the desert don't hate me after all.

\#

It don't take me long to lose my sense of optimism. We're down one goat, and that stings something awful. We tried to save her, of course. Pulled on her lead, dug, dug, dug. She was too deep, poor girl. We could've tried all day, but she'd have choked on the dust, long before we'd managed to git to her, if we managed it at all.

Givin' up on her ain't sittn' well with me, but the dead don't ask us to undo what cain't be undone. We gotta accept that.

My heart aches fer that stubborn goat, but from a survival kind of way of lookin' at things, what's worse than Reba's desert burial is the fact that one of her coffin mates is a piece of tin sheeting. We lost our sled.

"You know it wouldn't fit through the hole anyways," says Ro.

I kick at my bag. "Don't make its absence suck less."

"I'll be okay. My leg is better, really May."

I turn myself away from the sun, pretend its harsh rays are the reason fer my eyes to be waterin' up. After a moment, all I gotta say is, "Well, all right then. Let's git."

Gittin's all we cain do. Sun ain't gonna burn less if we stand here debatin' our woes.

We load Nessie up with some of our heavy baggage, but even with her help, my shoulders feel awful sore after a time with all that weight on 'em. When the heat of the day chases us off the path, we count ourselves fortunate to discover the side of a barn, still halfway standin', which provides a bit of shade and a place to lie against.

While we're restin', Ro consults his compass and unrolls his map.

"We've got to start heading south-southeast now."

"Why's that?" I stare down at his map. He's pointin' to one of a series of tiny black X's next to which have been scrawled some nearly incomprehensible words.

Ro smiles fer the first time since we set out the day before yesterday, and I find myself unaccountably reassured.

"Water."

It's Ro's belief that each X on the map is our daily means of salvation.

Ro done told me that old trader back in the north gave him locations fer water sources, but I didn't necessarily believe they was applicable to this particular stretch of desert. No one never passed by my farm to come this way, and I mean no one. Granddad always said its cuz there ain't nothin' but death waitin' fer folks out here. I'm tendin' to believe this was one of the few sober thoughts Granddad ever had, given our trials and tribulations so far, but Ro, he don't see it that way.

He's gonna lead us to the nearest X on the map, there'll be water there and that's that. Ain't no room in his head fer doubt. I've never been one fer blind optimism, but I keep my comments to myself. At least we have a direction to set our feet towards. We have a goal, whether it's real or just the invention of a no good trader who done wanna steer Ro to his death, and me with him.

By the time we spy what I suspect is that long sought fer X, Ro ain't walkin' so good. He's usin' a stick I found fer him a ways back as a make-shift crutch and I cain tell from the set of his jaw that he's hurtin'. We need water, shelter, and rest.

The land ain't flat here like it has been so far. Craggy orange rocks stick up out of the ground like hands of buried giants. Followin' Ro's lead, we head towards one of the biggest and circle it till we come to its southwest side. Despite the sun shinin' its end-of-day rays on that area of the rock, there's a section cut into its center still held in shadows.

"A cave." Ro lights our lantern. "Just like the trader wrote on his map."

I tug on Nessie's lead, and follow him inside. Sure 'nuff, after a long narrow passage that slopes down as we shove our way along it, the space opens up into a sizable cavern. The air's different here. Cooler, moister. I ain't used to the feel of that, but I take it as a good sign that we will indeed be drinkin' our fill tonight.

That's 'fore I spy them faces starin' at us from across the cave, of course. One by one, lights flicker on and the sounds of guns bein' cocked echo through the chamber. We just woke a whole band of armed folks.

Shit, I think. Cain't nothin' be simple fer us, even fer one night?

I grab fer Frank, but Ro moves in front of me, holds his hands up like he's just gonna let 'em take him down without a fight.

"Ro, move!" Frank tries to nudge him out of the way.

He ignores Frank and me, keeps his focus on the unknowns. I count nine of 'em. Nine. With Orin's Pa plus his lawfolk friends, they was a party of nine too. But no way it cain be them, cain it?

"Hello there," Ro calls out real cheerful. "We've just come here for water and rest.

We don't mean any trouble."

"Yer girl there looks like she means it." A woman steps forward. Her short cropped hair frames a face lined from years of desert livin' more than from age. She got herself a common way of speakin', too. Lawfolk is proper citizens of the Regions, and ain't no exceptions. Lucky ones. But this one, she ain't that. She's as unlucky as the next desert dweller.

"May, put Frank down." Ro is real even in his tone.

"I will not."

"Yer outgunned, Curlicue." The woman holds herself real steady. "What you gonna do, take out one of us while the rest fill you both with buckshot? Now I ain't inclined to tell a woman to listen to a man, but in this case, I may have to make an exception. Do as he says and put yer gun down. I'd hate to have to kill sich a lovely young couple."

I hold Frank up a mite longer while I debate her point, but I know she's right. Mostly.

"You ferget, even if you shoot us both, one of yous would still die in the process. So it seems I still have some leverage," I say. "Seein' as though yer the closest, it's probably you I'm most likely to hit, and I'd hate to have to kill sich a lovely old bat. So here's what I propose. Agree to let us have us some water, give us a corner we cain rest in, and I won't do no shootin'."

The woman blinks her eyes real fast. The corners of her mouth turn up a bit. "You got spirit, that's fer damn sure. It's a deal, Curlicue."

I lower Frank, everyone else holsters their weapons, and Ro and me git to the business of fillin' our canteens from a spring to the left of the cavern, all under the watchful eyes of them people. They ain't no lawfolk, so that's a sprig of good news. Still, I don't understand who they are, and why they're so protective of this here cave. Ro, though, he's got things figured.

"What are you trading in, if you don't mind me asking?" Dang it, why couldn't he have told me they was traders. And double-dang it, why didn't I figure that out myself!

The woman, must be their leader cuz she does all the talkin', answers in the kind of manner that ain't no answer at all. "Oh, this and that."

She do open up more to our non-work related inquiries. Her name's Tegan. Two of the youngest members of her group, maybe sixteen and eighteen, are her sons. She's from northeast of here, though she won't say where exactly. When she's not movin' what she swears is entirely legitimate merchandise through the desert, her favorite pastime is makin' pottery.

Well ain't that swell.

"Now it's yer turn," she says. "Seein' as though romantic liaisons 'tween commoners and proper folk happen this side of never, I'm guessin' the two of you have quite a story to tell." She looks at us real suspicious when she says it, like she already knows exactly what our story is.

"We don't need to tell you nothin'." I squint my eyes. Ro gives me a look like, come on, cut 'em a break here, May, and then he starts speakin' in his storyteller voice, the one you cain't help but listen to.

"What you need to know is that we aren't officers of the law, and we're not informers either. We aren't interested in the legitimacy of the goods you're carrying, nor do we want to steal those goods from you. In fact, we're grateful to you for sharing your space with us. We wouldn't have made it another night without this refuge." He taps his bad leg. "And as for who we are, well you've got it right. May here is from a different class, but none-the-less, I fell in love with her. Can you blame me?"

Tegan's oldest son whistles and says, "Ain't no way I'd pass her up, neither."

"Well," continues Ro, "my family didn't approve of our relationship. They ordered me to end it, but I refused. I said I'd rather be cast out into the desert than give up my love for her. And that's what happened. They cast us out. So here we are, traveling through, looking for a home where our love will be accepted."

Ro, he is a marvel. A couple of the traders smile, and one of 'em even dabs his eyes with his kerchief. Tegan nods, but ain't no way he's convinced her. She got a look that says she'll be keepin' an eye on us till the moment she witnesses our backsides crestin' the horizon.

Ro does git a response from her when he asks about the best course to take to git to the next X on his map. Unfortunately fer us, Tegan's answer ain't at all comfortin'.

"That map's terribly out of date." She studies it over Ro's shoulder. "Whoever made it ain't been in these part in a while. That one there, that one, that one too, all them water sources been dried up and fergotten about fer years now."

Ro and I exchange a look. His shoulders tense up. The cave, so spacious just a short while ago, feels like it's closin' in on me. "Ain't no goin' back the way we came. We gotta git through to south of the desert."

"Why south?" she asks.

I shrug. "Cuz it ain't north." That's the best answer I cain give, cuz truth be told, we don't have an actual destination picked out. We just wanna git through the desert and then decide from there.

"Hmm." Tegan turns away from the map. She don't offer us no advice.

After that, Ro and I settle into our corner of the cave along with Nessie, and the traders do the same across the way from us. Tegan may seem on the up and up, but even Ro ain't willin' to have us both sleep with them traders in the vicinity. I tell him I'll take first watch on account of the fact that his hurt leg's tired him out something awful. Besides, come to find our route south ain't got nearly as many water sources as we originally assumed—I don't know if I cain sleep with that information coursin' through my brain.

Keepin' a low glow in my lantern, I watch the traders nod off to sleep, one by one. Soon, there ain't nothin' but the sound of my own heartbeat thumpin' away, carryin' a hypnotizin' rhythm. I listen to it go, thump-thump, thump-thump, and 'fore long, I ferget our travelin' setbacks and do the stupidest thing I ever done. I let the exhaustion of the day thump-thump its way into my head, and without even realizin' it's what I'm doin', I fall asleep.

Ch. 10: Believers

"**G**it up both of yous." Tegan's sharp voice calls me out of my stupor. Her and her people got them guns trained back on us again. Frank ain't nowhere to be seen.

Ro is sittin' up, rubbin' his eyes. "What's going on?" He struggles to his feet.

What's goin' on is that while I've been busy neglectin' my guard duties, Tegan took it upon herself to become acquainted with the contents of our packs.

"Who are you?" Tegan gits real close to Ro's face. Her gun flashes silver in the lantern light. "And don't lie to me."

That's when I see what she got in her non-gun hand—a copy of Why the spread of the Desert Should Matter to You. She holds it real gentle, like it's liable to burst into flames if she ain't careful with it. One of her sons clasps the other copies to his chest.

Ro tries grabbin' at the one she's holdin'. "That's mine." Tegan waves it out of his reach.

"That might be the first truthful thing you've said today." She narrows her eyes. "Tell me, how is it that a pair of star-crossed lovers finds themselves in possession of ten whole copies of the most controversial piece of literature ever to make its way to light in this dark land of ours?"

I swallow hard, and Ro looks a mite shocked. "You're familiar with it?"

"Course I am," she snaps. "Ain't a trader alive that don't dream of comin' across one of these. The government's been destroyin' copies fast as they cain find 'em. And they've been confiscatin' presses even faster, just to make sure no one else gits to printin' more editions. Ain't too many of these left in circulation, which means each copy's more valuable than a whole carton of guns. But here you come with more of 'em then is believed to be unaccounted fer. So let me repeat my question. How is it that you have these?"

I look back and forth 'tween Tegan and Ro. Tegan's tremblin' a little. It's the first time she's appeared even remotely rattled. And that's when I realize it—that book means something to her. Ain't just its material value. She values its content.

"Cuz he's the author," I blurt out.

"May!" Ro is the cautious one now, not wantin' to reveal the truth of ourselves. But I don't see no way 'round it.

Tegan takes a step back. Her face scrunches up like she just ate herself a particularly sour pickle. "He wrote it." She laughs, but it don't sound too genuine.

"And printed it, too." I nod.

"I don't believe you." She spits on the ground.

"Good." Ro glares at her.

"Look here, Tegan." I let out a low breath to compose myself. "I'm trustin' you with the truth and that ain't no easy thing seein' as though the person who wrote and printed these booklets is a wanted man. If he gits caught, he'll be tried fer treason. Fer all I know, yer gonna march us out of here in the mornin' bound and gagged, drag us back to civilization and turn us in. So why would I tell you something that could git us killed, unless it was true."

Tegan looks us both over, and her eyes soften. "I always thought a desert dweller wrote it." She sounds a mite disappointed.

"His name was Amos Kennedy." Ro straightens himself up. Guess he figures now I've spilled the beans, ain't no point in denyin' his involvement. "Three of us co-authored the booklet, including Amos. He died trying to get the truth out."

"The press fire," Tegan whispers. Ro's eyes spark with surprise at Tegan's knowledge of that event.

He nods sadly. "The press fire."

"Well I'll be." She drops her gun, hands Ro's booklet gingerly to her son, and then does the most unexpected thing imaginable. She grabs both of Ro's hands, brings her head down to them like she's bowin' to a god, and murmurs, "Thank you."

\#

Ro is a folk hero. Course, nobody who ain't seen the paper with its picture of him and the caption readin' "Wanted fer treason, Rordan Farnes, age 21" actually knows who the author of Tegan's favorite publication is. But still, as the booklet circulated, so have the stories. Some people say the writer is the nephew of a Counselor who's willin' to defy his powerful and corrupt aunt in order to enlighten the masses. Others say it's a poor girl come up from the desert who taught herself to read so she could author this piece of truth. A few figured it out though, more or less, that it's a whole group of folks, lucky and unlucky, rich and poor, but all brave, willin' to risk their lives fer the truth.

Eventually, the booklet made its way 'round to the northern Regions and down into the areas on the outskirts of the desert where traders, includin' Tegan, got wind of it.

"I never saw no official copy till now, but I did git to read an unofficial one once." Apparently, cuz of the crackdown on printin' presses, people have been takin' it upon themselves to hand copy the booklet. "A trader from up north showed it to me. That's how come I knew fer sure what yers was."

Ro is a little beside himself by this point. He never imagined his little booklet made its way outside of the capital city, nor that it'd had sich an impact on folks. He's rightly proud, but it's emotional fer him as well, seein' as though all his friends died cuz of those twenty-six pages. I put my arm over his shoulder and he rests his head against me.

"You done a wondrous thing, young man," Tegan tells him. Ro squeezes his eyes shut real tight, like he cain't bear a compliment at this juncture. "This book is hope that things cain change. Everyone who hears about it, and the lucky ones who git to read it, they know that to be true."

There it is again—the lucky ones. Only now we ain't talkin' about the luck that comes from riches. No, this is the luck that comes from knowledge. And not just knowledge of the facts and figures laid out in Ro's booklet, but the understanding that people care about what's happenin', that with each new person this booklet touches, there's one more soul who don't want our world to be undone.

I take one of the copies and turn it to the very last page, the part Ro calls the conclusion. It's a passage I'm particularly fond of, havin' read it over several times since the day Ro first showed the booklet to me. I hand it to Ro and ask him to read the last few paragraphs out loud. After a minute's hesitation, he complies.

"Can the spread of the desert be stopped before it reaches the Regions' boarders?" His voice is clear and vibrant as he reads. Then he closes the booklet and continuing on from memory. "Can it be stopped before it overtakes our towns, our capital, our fertile valleys? Can we call it back, hold it in check and maintain a world that is both livable and alive?

"That depends on you. Our minds here in the Regions have grown as dry and inhospitable as the desert. We've ignored the human consequences of desertification so long that we've become accustomed to viewing those affected by it as inhuman. But if we do not create in ourselves a fertile mind filled with good will and tolerance for our desert dwelling brothers and sisters, if we are not willing to see beyond our own indifference, then the human consequences will be felt by us all.

"It doesn't have to be so. The common people whom you have been taught to ignore and loath have more knowledge of this crisis than you have. This is because they have lived it. Their knowledge is lost on us because we find no value in knowing the hardships of the poor. As a result, the class distinction we have fabricated to malign those who live outside the Regions has created a paradox in which we are blind to potential lifesaving solutions.

"We, the authors of this treatise, call forth the following—give up your prejudices. Leave the false security of your homes and visit the poor. Listen to their stories. Learn from them. Befriend them.

"Then, when you have united yourselves with the same ideals, rise up together, all of you, and battle against those that would keep you ignorant of your own inevitable demise.

"Live in hope. For if you can end ignorance, surviving the desert will be the smallest of obstacles to overcome by comparison. The desert may be stopped, or there may be a way to reopen the portal that brought our ancestors to this world so that we can escape it. This secret... these solutions may lie within the minds of a commoners. Don't overlook their capacity to save us all."

Ro lays the booklet down on his wool blanket. The cave is silent fer a moment.

"Live in hope." Tegan nods. "Them words changed me the first time I read them. Changed a lot of folks, I recon."

"I had no idea." Ro shakes his head. "I thought after the fire, people would think it was too dangerous to care about this."

Tegan gives him her hawk-eye look again. "It's too dangerous not to care."

Ch. 11: Hope Stretched Across a Sea of Dust

O ur change in fortune's downright confoundin'. As I look 'round the cave, all them traders workin' out travel details with Tegan and Ro, I recall my disbelief that Ro was real when he came out of the gulch that first day. That's how I feel now about all that's happenin' to us. I had been under the impression that I'm the kind of girl who gits stuck with an alcoholic guardian, slimy, gropin' men, and a dyin' farm and ain't nothin' I could do 'bout it to change my lot. But I was as ignorant as them folks in the Regions, thinkin' there was a real distinction 'tween people, that luck was something you was born with or without and that was that. Now I know—I'm the kind of girl who escapes a dyin' farm with a man who managed to find his way to me through a sea of dust. I'm the kind of woman who determines her lot.

And now, we've got more than just our determination and a scruffy goat to git us out of this desert. We found ourselves allies, just when we needed 'em. Seein' as though I have some trust issues, I hold onto a lingerin' doubt that Tegan truly is willin' to orchestrate not only our passage out of the desert, but also what Ro refers to as the dissemination of his booklet. Her plan is fer her trader companions to reroute. Ain't no cargo they're currently haulin' that cain compare in value to Ro's booklet, so now they got themselves a new priority.

Tegan says there are already copies of the copies in the north and northwest, and most likely some along the western coast as well. But folks in the other directions is still purdy much livin' in ignorance. Them traders aim to change that. Tegan's sons will take two booklets northeast to their home town. Two more will head with theirs directly East, a trader named Cheri will take two with her to her home near the southeast Region, and a sixth trader will deliver two more directly south.

Once all of 'em git where they're goin', they'll start writin' out copies and spreadin' the word. They'll give the copies to their trader friends, with the end goal of gittin' 'em across the borders into the Regions. I don't have to remind you how dangerous this'll be fer 'em, yet none of 'em flinch at Tegan's orders. They're livin' in hope, these traders, and hope's a powerful motivator.

The six traders leave, start walkin' in their intended directions. Tegan kisses each of her boys 'fore they go. "Take care of yer little brother, ye hear, Vlad?" she gives her oldest a quick hug and her youngest a knowin' wink. "Don't let him git into no trouble."

"All right, ma." Vlad squeezes her hand, then he and his brother is out of the cave and gone.

I look 'round, assessin' the situation. We got us two remainin' copies of the booklet, and three traders, includin' Tegan. "Yer no longer headin' south," she tells us. "Ain't nothin' fer you there."

I'm about to tell her that that's the point. We wanna find somewheres where there ain't nothin' and nobody who'll bother us. And besides, where is it she wants to lead us to that she thinks is so special?

Fer all I know, it's a lawfolk holdin' cell she's set her sights on. Soon as I open my mouth, though, Ro steps in. "What do you know that we don't, Tegan?"

Tegan smiles, gives Ro a motherly pat on his shoulder. "I know a way out."

"A way out of the desert, you mean?" I'm a mite confused, cuz I don't exactly consider this news. She is a trader after all.

She leans in towards us both. "A way out. To where the law won't never follow you. I know how to set you on the course of freedom."

#

We're takin' our remainin' copies west. Tegan, along with two more seasoned traders named Gina and Vern, will come with, cuz Tegan's real set on her goal of keepin' us from gittin' killed or captured. They promise there ain't nothin' more they wanna do than to help us, and with that grim determination buildin' up in 'em, it's hard not to believe in their sincerity. It don't mean we ain't nervous about the direction we're headin', though, especially Ro. I'm glad he still has enough sense left in him to question Tegan's plan.

"We're still too far north." Ro points to his map. "If we head west now, we'll end up less than three hundred miles south of the capital. That area's tightly controlled."

"I hear you, but the pass we need to take through the mountains is directly west. Once we're through, we'll start veerin' to the southwest, and that'll take us out to the coast right where I need us to be."

The coast. I still cain't believe that's where we're headed. I don't even know what to expect from the ocean, what it will sound or look like. Ro and I both expected we'd end up in some dusty outpost in the south, still well inland from the Regions. But here Tegan's aimin' us right straight at one of the Region's mid-coastal ports. Her plan is bold, I'll give her that.

"I gotta make it known, Tegan, that I think this plan of yers is real perilous."

"Well, cain you think of anything better?" she asks me.

"Not really."

"Then you'll just have to risk it, Curlicue." She checks her pack, makes sure everything's ready to go. "Have you been practicin' yer rich folks' talk?"

I sigh. "Yeah, course I have."

"What's that?" She cups her ear like she's strainin' to hear me.

"I mean, yes, of course I have been practicing." I do my best to imitate Ro's stuffy city accent.

Tegan nods and turns to attend to matters more important than her argumentative charge. Her plan relies on me passin' myself off as a proper rich lady, and that terrifies me more than all them hundreds of miles of travel ahead of us. But I aim to do it, cuz if it saves Ro and me from the lawfolk, it'll be worth all our efforts.

The seeds fer our grand escape plan started with a flier Tegan saw a few weeks back in a town well east of here. It was advertisin' fer recruits, what the sign called 'New Pioneers.' Them New Pioneers was needed fer a bold expedition. Now, that flier was in a commoners' town but it weren't meant fer no commoners. How it ended up there, I don't know, but something about it caught Tegan's eye, so she took it off the wall she found it on and kept it with her.

"I done almost fergot all about it, till I meet up with you. And then I got to thinkin', this here flier might be yer salvation." She flattens out the sheet of paper and slaps it down in front of us.

I stare at it, tryin' to make out the words in the creases where the ink's been rubbed off. When I read where they want their New Pioneers to do their pioneerin', I cain't control my shock.

"You want us to take a boat to some island on the other side of the world that I ain't never even heard of before? What makes you think we'd wanna go there?"

Ro nods in agreement, though his reasonin' fer stayin' on the mainland is different than mine. "How would I continue my work if I'm stuck on a remote island somewhere?"

"That's just the thing." Tegan's eyes open so wide, I fear they may pop out of her head. "That island is perfect fer yer work. You git past the officials at the dock by pretendin' you're a privileged young couple from one of the eastern Regions. They don't gotta know who you really are. Once yer on yer island, you cain spend as much time as you like copyin' that booklet of yers. A ship carryin' supplies will come once or twice a year, and you cain send back yer copies to be spread over the continent every time."

"But I'll be found out then, won't I? If I give them the copies to distribute, I'll have to tell at least one person on the ship about them, and they'll in turn tell the law about me."

Tegan shakes her head, points to the flier. "Not no one on this ship's gonna turn you in. This won't be the first time the Good Lady Margarethe's taken on illicit goods, so to speak. Captain's a good man, I hear. Been fightin' yer cause since before you even knew you had one."

I stare at the flier again. It says the Margarethe is due to set sail fer a newly discovered island at the end of September, which gives us a little over a month to git to the coast. And they need one hundred fifty upstandin' citizens of the Regions to sign on, especially farmers. The plan is fer them folks to create a tiny colony there.

"What makes you think they'd choose us fer this expedition of theirs?" I ask her. "Ain't they got tons of folks signin' up, wantin' to git off this sorry piece of dirt?"

"I heard the courier clerk talkin' about it with a customer when I first laid eyes on this flier. Sure, if they'd let commoners sign up, there'd be droves of desperate folks jumpin' at the chance. But rich folks is too comfortable. Them farmers still got fields that yield a bountiful harvest. Plus they got their society, their community. Ain't no reason fer 'em to give it up fer some far away island. That's why they was sendin' that flier out across the land. Had to widen their net to catch enough volunteers. And yer the farmer half of a healthy young couple set to make a new life and fill it with happy babies. Yer perfect New Pioneer material."

"But Tegan." I pull on her sleeve cuz she don't seem to really be listenin' to me. "They ain't never gonna let me on board. I'm just a commoner."

Tegan laughs. "Not no more, you ain't."

And that's when I start my lessons on how to speak like a proper rich lady.

Ch. 12: The Up and Left

"Can you please talk like yourself for a minute?" Ro turns a frustrated face towards mine. I'm walkin' alongside his new sled, which is actually one of Tegan's old ones, loaned out to us fer the duration of our trip west. Ro don't enjoy ridin' while the rest of us walk, but it ain't like we cain all pile on board and expect Nessie to pull us all clear to the sea. And, I'm sorry, but he'd just slow us down if he walked. His ankle might be better, but it ain't no twenty-five to thirty miles a day better.

"I thought you'd be pleased, Rordan," I say real snooty, trying to goad him into rollin' his eyes at me. Tryin' to make him laugh, if I cain. "Wouldn't you prefer it if I always spoke as though I'd been raised in upper-crust society?"

"No I wouldn't. And besides, it's creepy, hearing that voice come out of your mouth. I'm not used to it."

"Well git used to it," I tell him, revertin' to my normal speech. "Tegan's right. I gotta act my way onto that ship or her whole plan falls apart."

"Fine, I get it. But when it's just you and me, May, promise me you'll talk like you normally would."

"Well, of course, my dear. I wouldn't dream of doing anything my darling husband would regard as inauspicious."

Ro half-grins. It ain't no laugh, but I'll take it. "You're going to make it onto that boat, May."

I kiss him on the nose. We left the cave with Tegan and the others nearly a week ago, and I been practicin' the whole time. It's surprisin' to find myself havin' this much fun pretendin' I'm someone else. An actin' troupe traveled through my town a few years back and I was so taken with 'em, all their bright costumes and makeup, I couldn't help wonderin' what it would be like to run off and join their company. But I had the farm and Granddad to think of, so when the troupe moved on, I stayed put. Now, it's like I truly have done and joined 'em. I'm on the road practicin' fer my next role. And not doin' sich a bad job if it, come to think of it.

It sure is nice to travel with folks who know where they're goin' and how to git there. Gina and Vern each pull a sled loaded with supplies and goods. Despite their weight, the sleds glide with surprisin' ease over the land and accordin' to the traders, it's actually less strenuous to pull them sleds than to attempt carryin' everything' on their backs.

Them traders, they got their system down pat. They know where to go to find shelter at midday and they know where to find water and a safe place to sleep every night. I'm not sayin' it's a picnic walkin' all that way, but it ain't so awful as I thought it'd be. Most of my stuff rides on the sled with Ro, so my shoulders ain't so sore. And I'm enjoyin' the new muscles this desert is forcin' to grow on me, even if they ache something fierce by the end of the day.

After the rough patch we suffered at the beginnin' of our journey, I cain't believe how mundane the days is gittin'. Not another livin' soul makes an appearance, and Tegan assures us we ain't bein' followed. Ain't nowhere fer anyone tailin' us to hide, so I suspect she's right.

With no lawfolk in the area to fear, the days is all 'bout gittin' that much closer to our destination—nothin' more. I practice my rich folks accent, Nessie pulls Ro along over the dunes, and the traders add a safe and companionable presence to our journey. I'm hot and sweaty and sore, but I cain breathe again. And the desert, if it is awake, it don't pay us no mind.

Course, good days is bound to run out at some point. And when they do, they turn bad right quick.

#

We cross over into semi-arid land some two weeks after settin' out with the Tegan and her lot. This patch cain't but remind me of home. It's got that destitute feel to it, like it's someone tryin' to keep themselves from ruin, stay out of the poor house, quit drinkin'. But they just cain't, they cain't. One night they find themselves at the bottle and the next they got no home and nothin' to call their own. That's what this place is like. It's just about to crack that bottle open with abandon but it's still in denial about hittin' bottom the next mornin'.

Almost makes me homesick just thinkin' about it... Unlike home, though, there ain't no towns here, or no towns with people in 'em anyways. After a day's hike through the semi-arid zone, we find ourselves in a real and proper ghost town. Whole place has been abandoned, and no wonder. Anybody with a lick of sense cain tell this place is the desert's next meal.

"Everyone up and left three years ago," says Gina. She looks 'round with a sort of longing on her face, as if she got a stake in this shriveled little speck on the map. "Most of 'em are beggin' on the streets of the capital by now."

"This where you grew up, ain't it Gina?" She nods but don't say no more. I know better than to prod into a person's miseries, so I let the matter rest.

Winds is pickin' up speed again. The dust's alive and dancin', ready to jump its borders and kick apart this up-and-left town. Seems we're gittin' out just in time.

Past that town is our next aim—mountains with barely the remnants of snowcaps still clingin' to 'em in the end-of-summer heat. There's a pass through them, or so I been told. I cain't quite believe there's an easy way through, lookin' at their towerin' height hidin' the settin' sun directly to the west.

We set to pass the night in what used to be the town's boarding house. Fer the first time since we left the farm, Ro and I got us some real privacy.

"Finally." Ro closes the door behind him. I don't know how much time the people had to prepare 'fore they left this place, but they ain't took none of their stuff with 'em. I guess draggin' it all somewheres else wasn't too appealin'. Well, the point of me mentionin' it, is that this room of ours got itself a bed, and when Ro says "finally," ain't no mistakin' what he plans on doin' in that bed.

He pulls me over and gits to the business of takin' off clothes, both his and mine. "Ro, I got two weeks of dust on me."

But he don't care. "I'll take you just as you are." He nips at my neck. "If you'll do the same for me."

Dusty and road weary though he may be, he's still a sight I'd happily drink up any day.

"Well, you do smell something awful, but I suppose I cain be persuaded to see past it." Laughing, he hoists me up onto him, bare legs straddling his middle and then kisses me like I'm the first drop of water he's had all week. My arms and legs wrapped tight 'round him, dust pressed against dust, I let him carry me over to the bed.

The desert trail and all the sorrows we been carrying on ours shoulders is pushed aside. We let ourselves ferget fer a time that there's anything but the two of us, that there's still people in the world who mean us harm. We ferget that we ain't invincible, that what we have together is as delicate as a seedling struggling against the dust.

We let ourselves be at ease fer a time. That's most likely our first mistake.

Just as I'm driftin' off, one arm sprawled lazily across Ro's chest, the door gits a poundin'.

"Ro? May?" It's Vern callin' to us. "Tegan says she saw some people approachin'. Maybe three or four."

Ro is already out of bed, buttonin' his fly, grabbin' fer his boots. "Where?"

"Comin' up from the pass."

"I'll check it out," Ro tells me. Just like that we are back to our state of vigilance. I hand him Frank and search the floor fer my undergarments while Ro throws on a shirt. "Get all our stuff together, May, and meet me downstairs."

He slips out the door. Two sets of boots echo down the corridor and then I'm left with nothing but the howlin' of the wind. I run to the window, but it looks out to the north, not the west. There ain't nothin' but dust on the glass and more dust on the landscape beyond it.

'Fore long, everything's packed again and ready to go, in case we have to make a run fer it. I'm just about done strappin' closed Ro's pack when he surprises me by comin' back sooner than I expected.

"Well, Ro?" I secure a final buckle. "What's the word? We got anything to worry about?"

"No, dear, nothing to worry about." Low, cold voice. Ain't my Ro.

I swing 'round, but only git part way 'fore a big burly hand clamps down over my mouth. The stranger's other arm wraps 'round my waist, cinchin' my arms to my sides. I squirm as best I cain to try to wriggle my way free, but this man—he's strong. I let out a scream but not only is it muffled by his big meaty palm, he works his fingers over my jaw and squeezes it shut, hard. He keeps the pressure on, till I cain tell he's givin' me finger-shaped bruises on the lower part of my face.

"You've already said all you need to." He sounds like he just won a prize at the town fair, like manhandlin' a woman half his size is the most fun he could be havin' with his day. "There's no point in straining that voice of yours. Now, do as I say and you may just walk away from all of this. I'm going to take my hand off of your mouth and you're going to keep it shut. No noise. Nod if you understand me."

I don't know what else to do. Ro has Frank, so I ain't got no weapon. My attacker's standin' behind me and all he'd have to do is twist my neck just a little too far and that'd be the end of May June Stebbins. What cain I do?

I nod.

Slowly, the man lowers his hand. "Good girl." He steers me towards the door. "I'm going to assume when you called out for Ro that that is your pet name for a young man named Rordan." His hand is an anchor on my neck as we walk slowly forward. I keep my mouth shut just like he wanted me to, but now he gits a bit miffed about it.

"Rordan. Is that the name of your—companion?" His hand grips my neck now, pressin' into it until I wince. I don't respond, so he says, "Tell me now, girl!"

I won't. Now that I know he's here fer Ro, and not just to attack travelers at random, I got me an inclination to be as obstinate as possible. We reach the top of the stairs.

"Go to hell!" I cry and then stomp on his foot as hard as I cain.

"Bitch!" He's angry, but I've surprised him enough that he's loosened his hold. I jab my elbow back into his chest and then I run, takin' the stairs two at a time.

No sooner have I reached the first landing, then the man has recovered and is on me again. He flies down the stairs, slammin' me into the wall 'fore I cain turn the corner and keep goin'.

I cry out, catchin' myself with my arms to spare my head the worst blow. Then he's turnin' me 'round, grabbin' my wrists, and I think, Orin, that's how Orin got me. I start breathin' real fast and I cain't shut up with the screamin', even though he's orderin' me to, cuz all I cain think of is Orin on top of me, Orin with his tar-stained teeth and good-fer-nothin' grin. And here's another just like him. By the way he talks I know he's from the Regions, brought up real nice and proper, but he's still a brute, willin' to git what he wants by force. Ain't no difference 'tween the two.

Finally, this man, this proper speakin' version of Orin, decides just like Orin did, that he don't have to put up with me no more. He turns me to the stairs and pushes me down. I fall, tumblin' tumblin'. Cain't spare my head, nor any other part of me this time. I land on the lobby floor, all the air pounded out of my body. 'Fore I cain pick myself up and assess my injuries, the man is on me again, doin' the pickin' up fer me. He grabs me by the neck like he's a mama cat carryin' her kitten and yanks me to my feet. That's when I realize we ain't alone.

I search the room, dimly lit from the passin' of the day. Our trader friends, all three of 'em, are backed into one corner bein' frisked by two armed strangers. Apparently, while I was upstairs gettin' coerced by my oversized captor, his friends and mine were havin' it out. Gina's leg is bleedin', and Tegan's got a bruise formin' on her forehead. The strangers look less impaired. And not only that, they're nicely dressed, cleaner, and they got better weapons. Plus, two of 'em took out our three. These is folks with proper trainin', with fundin'.

Lawfolk.

The only person missin' from this equation is Ro. I say a silent prayer that he got away and that he'll keep goin'. It's him these lawfolk want anyhow. He should use the fact that they're distracted by the rest of us as an opportunity to escape. But I know Ro. He ain't leavin' me here with 'em, nor the traders who risked themselves to help him. That's why I'm not surprised when he comes 'round from a room behind us, holdin' Frank steady.

Ro and Frank, they do make quite a team. Unfortunately, one of them lawfolk has tossed my captor a gun, and by the time Ro comes into view, it's pointed at my gut.

"Put the gun down!" Ro shouts at him.

My captor, he's real calm, real scary calm. Every word out of his mouth is measured.

"When a hostage-taker points his gun at his captive, the traditional choice is to aim it at her head. But, I don't know, call me a free thinker. I prefer a gut shot. One blast to the head, and it's over and done with, practically before it's even begun. But if I shoot her here," he jabs me below the ribs, "well that gives her days to think about how things could have gone differently. That is, if she's able to think at all through the immense pain she'll be experiencing. Three, four days and if you're still here, you'll get to experience all of it with her. By the second day, she'll be begging you to end her life, and by the time her end does come, you'll barely be able to stand being near her, what with the overwhelming stench."

"I will kill you," Ro growls.

"Not before I shoot her, I assure you. However, there is a way to spare her life, to save her all of the agony I just described."

I already know what he wants, of course, and Ro does too, cuz he squeezes his eyes shut, and then holds his hands in the air, one of 'em still clutchin' Frank, now aimed harmlessly at the ceiling.

"No, Ro." I cain't believe he's givin' up. "Please no, don't do this!"

But it's already done. One of the lawfolk holdin' the traders steps over to Ro and takes Frank from him, then holds Ro's hands behind his back.

My captor drags me over to the traders so he cain be freed up to arrest Ro all proper-like. "Good job, Sargent Callan," the lawfolk now holdin' me along with my friends smiles at him.

Callan relishes every second as he coils rope around Ro's arms. Cuz if Ro ain't the biggest prize at the fair, I don't know what is. "Rordan Bennett Farnes, you are under arrest for crimes of treason and law evasion. You will be brought before the Council to stand trial. May the gods have mercy upon you." He moves to take him outside.

"No!" I yell again, tryin' to run forward, only to get struck by the butt of a lawfolk gun.

Callen stops to give orders to his two subordinates. "If she or any of the others move again, kill them all. If they cooperate, spare them." Then he looks at me directly. "Do not try to follow us. You will only bring trouble upon yourselves. Remember that I was merciful to you. I could kill you easily, and no one would ever find out. I have chosen to let you live, but only as long as you cease to interfere with the transportation of this fugitive. If you do not comply, I will enjoy watching you die as much as I will relish the sight of Rordan Farnes swinging from the gallows."

My muscles tense, urgin' me to attack again. Why, out of all the lawfolk in the land did Ro have to be apprehended by one crazier than Orin and his pa put together?

"Calm yerself, girl." Tegan takes my hand and pulls me back to her. I search fer Ro's clear blue eyes 'fore he gits marched over the boardin' house's threshold. There they are, starin' at me just like on the day we met. I remember there was something I couldn't place in them eyes back then. But I cain now. Now they tell me everything—everything I need to know.

If there's a force of good remainin' in this world it is cuz people like Ro exist. That's why the desert, sich a despicable foe fer most folks, does Ro's biddin'. That force he's got, it cain't help but be felt wherever he goes, on whatever land he sets foot upon. What I saw in his eyes that first day and didn't yet recognize—that was vision. Vision beyond seein', beyond words printed in a tiny booklet, beyond time. His vision is fearless.

Ro, he knows to do this. To let himself be taken. That's what I think as he slips away into the night. He knows his decision saved my life, saved Tegan's and Gina's and Vern's too. But there's something else beyond that lifesavin'.

Ro, he lives in hope.

Don't matter what that Sargent Callen says, we will come fer Ro. We will free him. Cuz what Callen don't know is that we got a powerful force on our side. They got a few guns, some fancy clothes, and the right of law. But we got the desert—the dust of folks who lived and breathed this land fer generations, all their lives, their deaths, their hopes and despairs. The total accumulation of life lived side by side with death. That's our force, that's our strength. I'm gonna wake the desert with every footstep I take till the dust rises up against Callen and his men.

And when that dust settles, the deserts gonna spare the fearless, the good, the just.

I no longer doubt it.

Ch. 13: The Marooned

They took our guns of course. They ain't that stupid. And they found where we was shelterein' Nessie fer the night so she's gone too. But they did leave us our food and water and some of our other supplies, so I guess there's that.

I thought fer sure they'd take Ro back through the pass, but no. Vern, who hides in the shadows and watches 'em while the rest of us is fixin' up our wounds, says they headed north. Probably plannin' to skirt the desert's edge up to a more northern pass, and then bring their prisoner back to the capital on the northwest coast.

Skirtin' the desert—this makes me smile, cuz it plays into my plans, but Tegan, she ain't so pleased.

"Don't they know there's a dust storm brewin'? We ain't gotta be dealin' with them lawfolk and a storm, plus we'll lose time travelin' north. We need to git you to that boat by the end of the month."

Maybe the blow she took to her head done her more harm than I thought cuz she ain't exactly makin' sense. "Ain't no point in goin' to that ship if Ro ain't with us, is there?"

Tegan frowns at me. "It's a terrible loss, and you know I'm fond of Ro, but his message cain be carried on without him. You cain do it,

May. You cain qualify to be a New Pioneer and you cain keep turnin' out copies of Ro's book from that island. They may hang Ro, and again, that's more awful than words cain express, but you cain send a message to 'em. Ain't nothin' that cain stop the truth, not even death."

"Cain you hear what yer sayin', Tegan?" I gotta grasp onto my wrists so I don't punch her. "They're gonna try him and execute him in front of the whole godsdamn planet. I ain't goin' to no boat till I git him back and if I have to go north by myself and pursue 'em by myself and kill Callen and his men by myself than I surely will. Cuz believe me, I'm livin' in hope—hope that I cain git Ro back. Hope that I cain keep him alive. Now, I though that's what yer plan was too, or am I wrong?"

Tegan looks down, her face set real hard. "I just don't want you goin' on a suicide mission."

"That ain't what this is, Tegan." I shake my head. I cain't expect her to understand what I know to be certain, that if I pursue my rescue of Ro, I'll be doin' what's right no matter the outcome. So, all I say is, "I gotta do this, cuz it's what's gotta be done."

"I'll go with you." Vern hops up from his seat on the counter and stands nearby, lookin' set in his decision. I feel a lump of courage well up in me, thanks to him. Vern's got more years on him than the rest of us, even more than Tegan, but he's brave and good hearted.

Gina's just about finished wrappin' up her leg. She got grazed instead of shot straight through, which makes her a lucky woman if ever there was one. "I recon I'll be able to keep up too." She gives a nod to me and Vern and I smile at her.

"Well here I thought I was in charge." Tegan's hands are on her hips but I cain tell she's partly proud of her crew of brave-hearted smugglers.

"Ro and I let you think you was in command only cuz it seemed like yer ego could use the boost."

Tegan lets out a throaty laugh and when that's done she sighs. "Curlicue, looks like Ro picked the right desert dweller to give his heart to. If you got a plan fer survivin' the storm, goin' weaponless against a bunch of well-armed lawfolk, and gittin' Ro back, I'd sure love to hear it."

#

It's like they want us to track 'em. That's what I think as we follow their footprints across the dusty plains. They ain't made no attempt to disguise their tracks, and even with the wind, their trail's still visible, like Callen purposely stomped along so the grooves in his boot soles would be a permanent fixture on the landscape. Either they don't believe we'll have the balls to follow 'em, or Callen is bettin' on us doin' just that.

I tell this to the others and they don't argue with me. "Callen's crazy, ain't he?"

Tegan nods. "I ain't seen a man talk like that never. It's like he was... like he was-," she struggles to finish her thoughts.

I think back to Orin. "Like he was playin' with his food?" I suggest and Tegan nods.

"Exactly like that. He's mad is what he is."

"So, you really think he wants us to find 'em?" asks Gina.

"I think he wants Ro to suffer as much as possible, and Callen, he may not be right in his head, but that head still works real cunnin'-like. He had me pegged fer Ro's sweetheart the moment he laid eyes on me."

"Why didn't he just kill you, then?" Vern wonders.

"Did you miss his fancy monologue where he explained the difference 'tween shootin' folks in the head versus the gut? Ain't no fun in killin' me outright. He wants to drag this on, torture us, and Ro most of all."

"Fer the record," says Tegan, "That's why I was aimin' to keep you from followin' 'em. It's what Callen wants."

"Don't matter." I shift the weight of my pack to my right shoulder. "What he wants, what he don't want. Only thing I'm interested in is that he gits what he deserves."

We push ourselves on through the night, guided by the moon and Callen's intentional carelessness. Tegan thought we should wait till morning to head out, but I know now she was only tryin' to prolong our overtakin' 'em, hopin' that the storm would come along in the interim and after that, we'd have to abandon the mission all together. I keep us speedin' along, though. My plan relies on us findin' Callen's group 'fore the storm hits. We ain't more than an hour or two behind 'em, and I have a feelin', we'll catch up to 'em whenever Callen wills it.

\#

Sure, 'nuff, Callen's will exerts itself on us just after dawn. We come up over a hill and there they are, just across the expanse, fixin' up their tents with extra layers of canvas so they cain ride out the storm at least partly protected. They got coverage to the east in the form of a long bolder restin' on the ground like a god dropped it there. I expect they feel it's passable protection seein' as though we're in the semi-arid zone, but I know it's woefully inadequate fer the size of the storm currently brewin'.

I set my eyes upon the east, to the risin' sun layin' itself across the desert. The dust's still a slumber, enjoyin' its last moments of rest 'fore the sun's glow awakens it, till it feels the heartbeats of the hopeful and speeds them to victory.

We're close enough fer Callen's lot to spot us if they was to look hard enough. That means it's time to put the next phase of our plan into action. I hand Tegan a piece of Nessie's halter.

"I don't like this, May." Tegan bites her lip. "Yer a brave girl, but still. I cain't see how this is gonna work."

"Just trust me and play yer part, Tegan. Go on now."

She frowns at me, but then she gits to it, bindin' my wrists in front of me. "Tighter," I tell her, "We gotta make this believable."

"Whatever you say."

That done, Tegan hands the rope to Vern, who looks at me real doubtful. "It's okay. Go on Vern."

Vern yanks my rope and off we go, across the tableland and into Callen's trap.

Ain't no sign of any of 'em, but I know they're here. Once we're in earshot, Tegan yells, "Sargent Callen, we got you something you might be interested in."

Slowly, the flap at the front of one of the tents lifts up, and Callen steps out. "Well, now, I didn't expect to see you four again, and," he cocks his head at me, "what could that pretty young lady have done to earn such ill treatment?"

"After you done run off with her boyfriend, this one here," Tegan looks at me accusingly, "starts blabberin' on and on about how Ro ain't the real outlaw. How it was her all along who wrote them books. How Ro, he just took the fall fer her cuz they was in love."

Callen scratches his beard thoughtfully. His two men come out of their tents, armed with them fancy city guns. "She's a commoner." Callen spits it out like it hurts his throat just to say the word. "Do you really think I'd believe she's capable of writing anything? Most likely, she can't even read."

"I'm quite positive you've underestimated me, Sargent," I say in my very best proper talk. "And if we're speaking of what you do and do not believe, I must include that I'm quite certain I convinced you to believe exactly what I wanted you to."

Callen's eyes widen. Could he really be buyin' my act? If he does, he don't mind overly much that I duped him. "If that's the case, you're a bigger fool than Rordan Farnes. You had only to hold your tongue and you could have remained free."

"I love him!" I gush fer all it's worth. "I love him and I couldn't bear losing him!" I raise my bound hands to my face and brush away tears—tears that don't take too much coaxin' nor actin' skills to git out of me.

"So," Callen turns back to Tegan, "I must admit I didn't expect this turn of events. Why have you brought her here?"

"Ain't it obvious?" Tegan scowls at him. "To turn her over to you and collect whatever reward they're offerin' fer traitors these days."

Callen raises an eyebrow. "Who says there's a reward?"

"The fact that you and yer men were out in these parts, dealin' with this sorry stretch of land tells me it. Or was you lookin' fer fugitives purely out of a sense of patriotism?"

"I'll have you know, this 'sorry stretch of land' is my regular patrol. And yes, every officer from shore to shore knows to be on the lookout for Farnes. The fact that I caught him is-"

"Is yer ticket out of here," concludes Tegan. "You know very well they'll promote you, send you back to the Regions, give you a nice house and yer pick of easy-as-pie jobs. Well, that's all we're askin' of you. One traitorous love-struck girl fer a ticket to the Regions. As proper citizens. Promise us that and we'll help you git 'em both back to the capital."

Callen looks the three traders over. I cain tell he wants to say "yes" cuz it'll make him seem like he's got the authority to grant sich grand requests. And this man, he wants authority, or at least the appearance of it.

"All right. I'll entreat the council to grant citizen passes for your service to our land." He motions fer Vern to hand me over.

Vern tugs on my lead, forcin' me in Callen's direction. The prisoner transfer complete, Callen examines the traders like he ain't sure exactly what he ought to do with 'em now.

"Do you know what marooning is?" This is sich an out of place question, no one finds the words to respond, so Callen does the respondin' all on his own. "It was a punishment unleashed by pirates, people who used to terrorize coastal populations. Plundering, pillaging, that sort of thing; pirates, in one form or another, can be found in the history books of many of the known realities from which our peoples spring. If a pirate defied his captain, the punishment was harsh indeed. The captain would sail to a tiny island and deposit the offending man there, leaving him with nothing other than a small but crucial parting gift-- a gun containing one solitary bullet. The marooned man would slowly die of thirst and when he could bear his fate no longer, well, he'd consider that gun a true gift of mercy."

Callen turns towards his men. "Take all of their supplies. If they try to defy their new captain, we'll withhold food and water, situate them in the middle of the most inhospitable spot we can find and leave them there."

He smiles at the traders. "Without a gift of mercy, obviously."

He leaves the traders to contemplate why they was fool enough to go along with my plan. Next thing I know, I'm bein' tossed into a tent. I'm hopin' badly that Ro will be there, but of course, that'd be too easy, wouldn't it.

"Where's Ro?"

"Relax, dear." Callen's got the nerve to pat my head. "Your boyfriend's unharmed. They want him alive for the trial."

"I want to see him."

Callen looks me up and down. "No, I think it best you two stay separated as much as possible. You understand, don't you?"

"I understand plenty, just not a whole lot when it comes to you."

"Well, I love to keep a lady guessing." Callen checks the rope bindin' my wrists and then secures me to the tent's center pole before turning to leave. "I'd get some rest, if I were you. We have weeks of travel ahead of us."

No we don't, actually, not together, at least, but he don't know that yet. I shut my eyes and let my head rest against the pole. I hope Tegan and the others will be all right. They put a lot of trust in me. If I was them, I'd be havin' serious doubts about that choice right about now.

But I cain't think in terms of doubts and worry. I gotta be fearless. Even now, the wind's pickin' up its pace. The desert's ready fer us. It's famished, and I know what will settle them hunger pains.

I got some things to figure out and not a lot of time to do it. Fer one, I need to know where Callen stashed our guns. Also, I gotta know where Ro is. And finally, it'd be real helpful if I wasn't tied up in this tent.

"Callen," I call out. "Sargent Callen!"

The tent flap opens but it ain't Callen who comes in, it's one of his men. He's young, maybe even younger than me, with strange orange tinted eyes set close together. He looks a little too excited 'bout the fact that there's a young lady all tied up and helpless right in front of him.

"What do you want?"

"Oh, I'm so glad you're here." I barely remember to keep with my proper accent. "What is your name, officer?"

He closes the flap and crouches in front of me.

"Blaine."

"Blaine. I must ask you something indelicate."

He raises his eyebrow. "You've got to relieve yourself, miss?"

I let out a huge sigh. "Yes, thank you. I wasn't sure what I should do. I've never been held prisoner before." I look up at him through my eyelashes and smile.

Blaine gulps. "Sargent Callen told me not to untie you, no matter what."

"You can keep me tied up, if you'd like." I bat my eyelashes, keep my smile real wide. "Just lead me out behind the tent and turn around. Or don't turn around, if you prefer. Won't that be okay?"

"Well, I mean... yes, but." He's gittin' ready to cave, orders be damned. I'm gonna win him over, cuz Blaine's got everything I need him to have—a gun, a knife, and an overabundance of hormones.

"Maybe if we call your Sargent, he'll be able to tell you what to do."

"He's busy with those desert traders. He won't want to be bothered."

Perfect. "Then can't we go real fast? I'll be back here before he even knows I was gone. And then I'd owe you a favor. You'd like that wouldn't you? If I owed you something?"

Blaine looks back and forth like there's someone else in the room that cain make the decision fer him. But I've tempted him with something he ain't likely to resist. Finally, he comes 'round.

"I suppose I would like that." He keeps my arms bound, but unties me from the post and then drags me outside and 'round the back of the tent fer me to do my business. 'Fore we git there, I chance to look beyond the lawfolk tents to where a new one's sprung up. Must be fer the traders. Shadows pass back and forth in front of the soft light glowin' from within it. Hopefully, Callen's still inside there, occupied with Tegan.

"Here we are." He comes to a halt. "You know, I'm going to have to watch, just to keep my eye on-"

That's as far as he gits, cuz I've taken the rope tetherin' me to him and looped it 'round his neck.

Blaine chokes and sputters, graspin' at my makeshift noose with his hands. "I don't wanna kill you, Blaine. But I will unless you do exactly what I say. Got it?" His eyes bulge. Oh, he gits it all right.

Blaine nods slightly. "I'm gonna let the rope loosen just a bit." The wind roars 'round us, so I say my words real firm in order to be understood. "And yer gonna keep yer mouth shut, you hear me?"

He nods again. "You know how I know yer gonna do as I say, Blaine? Cuz while we was walkin' back here, I took the gun you was carryin'. You know, it ain't too smart to have a gun down the back of yer pants when yer escortin' a prisoner behind you. I kind of git the feelin' you'd be reprimanded by Callen fer that."

Poor Blaine, he looks like he might just cry. I almost feel sorry fer him. He's just so dang green, me liftin' that gun without him even realizin' it. Stupid. I thought they trained lawfolk better than that. "I'm gonna loosen up on you now, and as long as yer quiet, I won't kill you. And keep yer hands up high."

Lettin' go of the rope, I move 'round so that I'm facin' him fully. My gun stays level with his face. I'd like to take his knife from him next, but my hands are still tied together and I'd have to lower the gun to git at it. And I cain't very well ask him to cut through the rope fer me, cuz it'd be way too easy fer him to grab the gun out of my hands. No, I'll have to deal with remainin' tied up fer now, and just focus on gittin' information from him.

"Where's Ro?" He don't say nothin'. "Where's Ro, or I'll shoot a hole 'tween them beady eyes of yers."

"Why are you talking like a commoner? I thought you were from the capital." He stares at me through them weird eyes. Damn it. Maybe I'll have to kill him after all.

"Last chance," I say, cockin' the gun.

Ain't no denyin' I mean business. "All right! All right! He's in the tent with the orange flap."

The lawfolk have three tents—the one I was in, a smaller one with a grey cover, and a final one next to that, sportin' a bright orange door. "Good, we're finally makin' progress. Where's Frank?"

"Frank?" He's all confused.

"Frank, my shotgun." I growl at him, and the desert echoes. Dust swirls 'round our heads, pricklin' our eyes. Both of us squint, tryin' to keep it out. "And my goat and all the supplies you took fer that matter."

Just like she heard me talkin' about her, Nessie's panicked bleatin' overpowers the wind's cries. Peerin' 'round Blaine's shoulder, I cain just make her out through the dust-darkened air, wedged between two tents along with the sleds carryin' our supplies.

"Callen's got your guns," Blain claims. "I don't know where they are."

"Well, one thing at a time, I suppose." I push him in front of me and we round the back of the covered grey tent, and then approach the third. If Blaine's tellin' the truth, Ro should be right inside. But the entrance is clearly visible from the traders' tent. If Callen were to spy me tryin' to git Ro out, we'd be in big trouble. Like the maroonin' kind of trouble.

I crouch down with my head next to the back of the tent, still aimin' the gun at Blaine. "Ro? Ro, you in there?"

No response.

"Blaine, take yer knife and start slicin' the canvas."

He looks surprised. I wonder how rich a person's pa has gotta be fer someone as clueless as Blaine to land a job as an officer of the law. Don't they gotta pass some kind of intelligence test or something? The kind of test that would have questions like, "If an underfed smart aleck desert dweller steals your main weapon, what do you do?" Poor Blaine must have missed that one, cuz he's fergotten till now that he's had himself a sizeable knife at his disposal this entire time.

I stand up and take a step back from him, so I'm too far away fer him to stab. My gun stays steady. "Go on then," I coax. "Knife. Canvas. Slice."

Blaine wrinkles his nose at me, causin' his eyes to move even closer together. Then he sets to slicing.' 'Fore long, he cries out in alarm, and poor stupid Blaine, he's bein' sucked inside the tent through the hole he just made. I cain't tell why or how it's happenin', but I cain guess.

Blaine's still halfway out of the tent, his legs kickin' as he tries to scramble backwards. I shove his backside, willin' him forward, cuz he's blockin' my way to Ro.

Blaine loses the fight with his assailant and the rest of him disappears into the tent. I follow close behind, only to find myself inside a dim space with a knife pressed to my throat.

"Ro!" My voice breaks over the dust I've been inhalin'. "It's me!"

If I had to go on sight alone, I wouldn't have known who I was dealin' with. It's too dark now, and we're nothing but shadows to each other. But it's him. His breath comes in heavy gasps. I reach out and there's his hand, still holdin' Blaine's knife. He begins to shake as he clasps onto me, onto the reality that it's not some demon come to torment him.

"May? May?" He leans his head against mine, and we're both tremblin' now.

"It's me." I desperately wanna throw my arms 'round him, 'cept both of us still have our wrists bound. I kiss him, and he cain't help but wince. His lip's been split. Well, we ain't got time fer that kind of reunion anyways. Blaine lies a few feet from us, moanin'. "Git these bindings off me, then I'll help you."

Ro works clumsily, tryin' to cut through my ropes in the darkness, his own hands still locked together. "How did you...? When did you get here? Where's Callen?"

"Tegan and the others are keepin' him distracted. I had her convince him I was the real outlaw—that you was just coverin' fer me. Callen arrested me and secured me in another tent. We've been here fer hours already. Didn't you know that?"

"No, I've been—I guess I've been unconscious." His words are so soft that the noise the world's inflictin' on us threatens to drown 'em out. "There, you're done."

I shake out my sore wrists and then take the knife from him. "What did Callen do to you?"

"I tried to get away. He got angry. Look, it's nothing, May. I'm fine. But we've got to get out of here."

"Agreed." I git to cuttin'. "And fer that, we need our guns back."

Ch. 14: The Desert's Last Meal

Ro ties Blaine up to the same pole he himself was secured to just a few minutes ago. We wrap our scarves 'round our heads to protect us from the dust as much as possible, and then head out of the hole at the tent's back. I use Blaine's knife to slice through the back of the grey tent, cuz ain't no other place fer our guns to be stashed. Inside is all of their supplies. They got their own sled with a couple crates loaded on it, and there's a couple of bedrolls where Callen's men must've intended to ride out the storm.

Like hell Blaine didn't know where our guns were, cuz even in the odd blackness of the day, I cain feel my way along the perimeter of the tent and, not three feet from them bedrolls, there's a fold of canvas containin' all our guns.

"Frank," I clasp the shotgun to my chest. "Oh Frank, I never thought I'd see you again."

"Should I be jealous?" Ro grabs the traders' weapons.

"Havin' both of you back just about makes my life complete."

"Help!" a voice brakes over the desert's howl. "They got me, Sargent, help!"

"Seems Blaine woke up." I grin. "Right on schedule."

We stand on either side of the tent's openin', listenin' to Blaine whine. The stomp of boots rushin' by follows. "Now," I mouth to Ro 'fore lifting my kerchief over my nose and slippin' from the tent.

We step out, just as Callen and his man enter the one Blaine's tied up in. To our right, Tegan, Vern, and Gina rush over to us. Ro tosses them their guns.

"I cain't believe yer plan worked, Curlicue." Tegan, eyes obscured behind goggles, shakes her head. She hands a pair to both Ro and me. I'm unaccountably excited to put mine on.

"Well, it ain't worked yet." I motion to the tent, out of which three very angry lawfolk emerge.

Vern takes a shot without hesitatin'. It wings through the tent, near enough to Callen's head fer him to display a certain amount of alarm. Callen's got a gun, and so does his other man, but we've got four, includin' Frank, and they're all ready to fire.

"Frank here was just mentionin' to me how it's been too long since he killed a man," I shout through my scarf, through the dust and the whippin' wind. "He's practically beggin' fer me to let him do it again. And if you don't drop yer weapons right now, I'm gonna give him what he wants."

Callen ain't a man to back down. He keeps his gun up, but his men ain't so fearless. Blaine ducks back inside the tent, and the other man wavers. We gotta finish this up soon. The storm ain't gettin' better 'fore it gits a lot worse.

"All right Vern, this time, don't aim fer the tent."

Vern angles his gun all menacin'-like and Callen's man drops his weapon and raises his hands. So much fer all their fancy trainin'.

Callen sighs deep and then, finally, he lowers his gun. "This isn't over."

"No, it ain't," I agree with him. "I promised the desert it could pass its final judgment upon you. So believe me, when it's over, you'll know it."

Gina and Ro collect the officers' fallen guns.

"Let's git our stuff and go," I tell my friends.

"You are a crazy woman," Teagan says. "Let's tie 'em up and ride out the storm in our tent."

"We cain't do that, Tegan. The desert's takin' this camp fer itself. If we're here when it comes, it'll take us too."

Ro puts his hand on my shoulder. "What are you talking about, May?"

"We gotta go. Now. Or we die. I know it to be true." Ro nods. He trusts me, even if I ain't makin' very much sense at the moment. I turn to the traders. "Ain't got no time to take the tent with us, neither. If you don't wanna come with me, yer welcome to share the fate of these lawfolk."

I don't leave no more time fer discussion. Runnin' over to Nessie, I tie a kerchief 'round her nose and try to comfort her with a few pats. "You gotta do yer part now, Nessie."

Ro helps secure her to the sled. "You able to travel?" I ask him, though I doubt I'll git an honest answer.

"Of course I am." I don't argue, cuz he's got no choice anyways.

#

After securin' the three lawfolk inside one of their tents, the traders catch up to Ro and me. I'm pleased to say they was convinced to vacate Callen's camp by my gloom and doom rantin'. We drag our stuff south, back towards Gina's ghost town and the pass beyond it.

Every step we take is more labored than the previous. Dust pelts our skin, and ain't nothing visible more than a few feet ahead of us. But I paid attention as we came this direction the first time. I know where we're goin'.

We huddle together, as if our closeness will drive off the dust. Ro pulls Nessie along and we go fer what feels like a long stretch, though I know we ain't too far from where we started.

"We cain't just keep on like this, Curlicue." Tegan struggles with her gear.

"We won't. I promise." A few minute later, I move us off to the right a bit. The land starts to climb. Higher and higher, we go, till there's just the slightest lessonin' of the wind. The terrain is rough here. Ain't no path nor light to make our way easier. Ro's ankle gives out twice, but I keep him upright, and we carry on. Once we reach the top of the hill, I turn to the others.

"Here we are. I know it's dark, but we gotta feel our way over to the west side a bit. We cain lay low there. Wait out the worst of it."

And that's what we do. We find a slope, lower ourselves and our stuff down it, and take shelter. It cuts off enough of the storm's power that we cain hope more air than dust is workin' its way into our lungs.

Ro slumps against me breathin' hard. I rest my head on the top of his, our hands interlace. I don't need no light to know his face is all beat up. I'd be mad, 'cept I'm certain the desert's justice is already at work. Callen's payin' fer doin' this to Ro, and I ain't sad 'bout it.

"You risked your life to come for me." Ro turns his face to mine. "I knew you would."

"That's cuz you know I love you Rordan Bennett Farnes. Ain't enough lawfolk in the world to keep me from you."

Ro is quiet fer a moment—so quiet I start to think he's fallen asleep. 'Fore I nod off myself, he finally says, "I don't know what I did to deserve you, May."

"You put truth into the world. You took the world's worst enemy and woke it to the reality of our strife. You saved a starvin' desert girl from her own personal hell. What you deserve is more than I could ever possibly give you."

"You give me everything, May. Everything."

I hold him against me and he does the same. The rage of the storm cain't touch us no more.

"Are we gonna go back fer them when the storm passes?" Gina asks. "To untie them, I mean?"

"Maybe," Tegan says without commitment.

"Ain't you figured things out yet?" I ask 'em. "When the desert's done with them lawfolk, won't be nothin' fer us to go back to."

After that, they don't say no more and when, after hours of givin' us its worst, the storm finally does pass, no one even looks back towards where the camp used to be 'fore the desert swallowed it whole.

Ch. 15: Chosen by Spirits

S eems we'll always be lookin' over our shoulders. Could be Callen and his boys on our tail again, could be other lawfolk -- that's what the others think at least. I ain't so naive as to reckon we're home free, but if we're being followed, it ain't Callen who's on the chase. Ro's been educated in the ways of the desert. He believes in its spirit the way children believe ghost towns really got ghosts in 'em. So it don't take him long to figure I know what I'm talkin' about when I say the desert has done in our former captors once and fer all. He just looks at me and nods whenever Tegan questions him on it. "If May says they're dead, then they're dead, Tegan. Callen won't be bothering us again."

Maybe Callen won't be, but we all figure that lawfolk in every corner of the continent aim to bother us if they cain. We got ourselves out of a mighty jam, but that don't mean another one ain't waitin' fer us around the next bend. And purdy soon, we won't have the desert to help us git rid of our law-abiddin' burdens.

'Fore you know it, we're through the semi-arid zone with its familiar misery and on to the mountain pass. It's an alien land of grey and white—sich a different sort of severity then the kind I was raised with on the edge of the desert. The tips of my fingers ache as I scoop up snow from what Gina says is the remnants of last winter's ice pack. I hold it gently, like it's a hen's very first egg, until it's all but melted to a tiny pebble. I place that bit on my tongue, but it ain't got no taste to it.

And then it's gone.

It cain't help but make me think of home, of how my farm and the land beyond it has been savorin' its own remnants from a time when rain came with a seasonal regularity. The drought's been with us fer years, but we're still dwellin' on that past. When that remnant dries up, it will slide into memory, and people will have drunk up their last drop without realizin' that's what they was doin'. Don't matter how long they've had to git used to the idea, it'll still be too late.

I gotta turn my mind away from the farm, from everything that's behind us now. I'm lookin' to the west. Cuz it's August, the mountain pass ain't as formidable as I thought it might be. It'd be easy fer that twisty trail to take a life come winter, but right now, it's just another obstacle and it don't seem nearly as difficult to overcome after what we've been through already. We push past them towers of stone on into a new world so green my eyes water just thinkin' 'bout it. To be in a land full of life—you ain't got no idea the wonder of sich a thing unless you was raised without it. All sorts of plants grow on the west side of the mountains, in the Southwest Region. They don't need no coaxin', no pleadin'. There's whole fields of wild berries, streams runnin' with fish, trees laden with fruit and nuts. Ain't caused no one much effort at all to make it that way.

I could stay in them valleys ferever, 'cept of course, it ain't safe fer us here. The traders move Ro and me through at a steady pace. The closer we git to the coast, the more nervous we all become. We gotta be on the lookout fer lawfolk—lawfolk with just as much cause as Callen to wanna send Ro and me swing from the gallows.

We travel at night, hide ourselves durin' the day. One time, as we're shelterin' in the loft of an old barn, we're very nearly found out. In fact, we are found. Tegan raises her gun at the sound of someone climbin' a ladder up to our hidin' spot. But it's just a little girl, maybe five or six, her eyes grown wide at the sight of us.

"We're spirits." A sing-song voice in my proper Regions accent fills the loft. "We've chosen to appear before you, and that makes you very special. Your life will be filled with blessings, and you shall always eat as much honey as you wish."

The girl giggles and I place my hand on her head like I'm givin' her my blessin', all personal-like. "Only you mustn't tell anyone you've seen us, my dear. The magic will be destroyed completely if we are not kept a secret. Do you understand?"

She nods, promisin' me through a gap-toothed smile that she won't tell no one, and I dismiss her, hopin' that if she does blab, all her talk of spirits will be thought of as nothin' more than childish imaginings. We ain't dependin' on that though.

As soon as her downy head disappears below the rafters, we gather our things and you best believe we remove ourselves from them premises about as fast and gracefully as us tired-out spirits cain manage. I run alongside the others, my heart beatin' hard out of fear as well as our quickened pace, expectin' all the while to hear the barkin' of dogs or the hollers of angry men as they close in on us. It's broad daylight and we're frightfully exposed, so if they're lookin' fer us, they'll find us. But the girl, it seems she took me at my word, sorry excuse fer a spirit though I may be. We are a magical secret she'll cherish keeping, at least as long as no one denies her that sticky goodness from her family's hives.

The nearer we git to the coast, the more often we find ourselves within shoutin' distance to lawfolk patrollin' our area, searchin' fer criminals sich as ourselves. Our most white knuckled brush with the law occurs early one morning, less than one hundred miles from our goal. While he's off scoutin' ahead of our group, Vern nearly runs into a couple of soldiers.

"Them lawfolk came out of nowhere, I swear," he tells us later on. They come around a bend and Vern has no choice but to throw himself into a conveniently placed but unfortunately thorn-filled ditch in order to go unnoticed.

If it weren't fer the fact that Vern's about as wily as they come, them soldiers would have met us dead on a mile or so from that point. But Vern, he takes off through the woods, blood red and berry purple from head to toe thanks to the brambles he'd recently become acquainted with. And damned if he don't beat the law back to where we're camped out awaitin' his word.

After several frantic minutes of gatherin' ourselves together and coverin' our tracks, we watch from a distance as the officers march right on past. One of them pauses fer a moment, holds his hand out to motion the other to stop. He sniffs the air, and his friend does the same, but with an annoyed look, like he don't wanna be bothered with the fact that his partner's actually trying to do his job. They both inhale, and I do too, but I don't know what it is they think they'll git a whiff of. Fer gods' sake, we ain't dumb enough to light fires this close to the patrols, so it ain't smoke they're sniffin' at. Unless you're a hound dog, ain't nothin' to smell.

It's just a coincidence, I tell myself. That officer is of the opinion that he scents something peculiar, but it ain't got nothin' to do with us. Move along boys.

Ro holds his breath beside me. My shoulder may never fully recover from the squeezin' he's givin' it. Several of us, we got our guns aimed, just in case, but firin' upon them men is a last resort if ever there was one. Who knows how many folks would hear the sound of one of our bullets bein' launched towards its target. Announcin' our location to all those in the general vicinity—that we surely do not need to be doin.'

The lawfolk walk around in circles. They ain't exactly at the spot we'd been camped out on, but they're close, whether they know it or not. Finally, the impatient one lets out a sigh so loud ain't none of us miss it. His partner starts to protest, but then again, it's not like they turned up anything worth investigatin'. So they move on. When finally they're out of sight, I pry Ro's fingers from my shoulder, give him a reassurin' pat and, with a renewed cautiousness, we continue on our way. Vern becomes the day's official hero.

During our entire time travelin' through the Southwest Region, two lawfolk nearly disrupting our camp is as dangerous as it gits, believe it or not. Nobody aside from that little girl in her pa's hayloft actually finds us when we don't wanna be found. Callen don't rise up from the grave to seek his vengeance. No one comes fer us. No one of consequence, thanks to Vern, catches us completely unawares.

The desert's luck carries us all the way to the sea.

When most people set their gaze upon the ocean fer the first time, that big stretch of endless water ain't quite conceivable to 'em. All caught up in the roaring surf and the feel of real sand 'tween their toes, they're bound to say they ain't never seen nothing as blue as the sky till that point.

But I have.

Ro's eyes gleamin' against the dust—cain't no other blue compare. It's what the ocean and the sky wish they was—the purity of a person's soul brought out to shine forth to the world. My eyes ain't blue, they're brown, brown like the dirt. I tell this to Ro and of course, he has a response. "They're like the earth, May, the earth after it rains, when it's ready to call up life. Your eyes are the fertile world."

Well, when he says it like that....

We approach the port at night, and we are barely in time. As Tegan had warned, the excursion with Callen and his men delayed us nearly to the point of failure. Had we arrived but two days later, we'd have come to the port only to watch the Good Lady Margarithe sailin' over the horizon without us.

Once in the bustlin' town surroundin' the port, I find us a place to stay until sign-up begins the followin' afternoon. I do all the talkin', nice and proper-like, while Ro and the rest wait on the outskirts of town. It's risky enough fer Ro to show his face down at the dock when he'll have no choice but to. Ain't no point in him shinin' that grin of his around all them people linin' the walkways and fillin' the taverns. It wouldn't be no surprise to have someone figure him fer a match to the man on the wanted flier that've been widely circulated in these parts.

Sure enough, what do I spy but one of them fliers tacked up to the wall behind the clerk's desk at the boarding house. Its yellow edges are curled up, and it's partly covered by the same New Pioneer's ad Tegan has in her possession. Don't look like anyone's paid much attention in recent times to its dire warnin' about a dangerous traitor roamin' the land, but it sure does make me glad I left Ro behind with the others. I gotta calm myself, git my breathin' out nice and steady, cuz Ro will be out in the open come tomorrow. One keen-eyed lawfolk is all it'll take fer all our hard work gittin' here to amount to squat.

The inn is full thanks to all the potential New Pioneers temporarily taking up residence at the port, but the clerk does let me rent an old supply shed down the road. He does so apologetically, and I have to remember to cringe like a Regions lady would at the prospect of sleepin' on the floor of a shack. In truth, it's the best shelter we've had since ferever. The shed ain't got but one high-up window, and it's well outside of the busiest parts of town, which will suit our band of illegals just fine. Once the clerk leaves me by my lonesome in our luxurious quarters, I go and gather Ro and the traders. Only Ro will be comin' back to the shed with me, though, cuz Tegan announces that it's time fer them to say their good byes -- not before they give us two last surprises, though. The first is tied to Gina with a hemp cord.

"I figured yer goat there could use a friend." Gina hands the leash over to Ro, who steps back so that Nessie cain git to the business of buttin' heads with her new acquaintance. I gotta smile at this, cuz a lone goat is a sorry sight, and Nessie's done her fair share of gittin' us this far and then some. She deserves a new companion. Reba comes to mind 'fore I cain help myself, but I gotta drown out the thoughts that come with her – granddad's passin', my parents, the farm, Orin and his pa, everything that got taken from me and everyone who did the takin'. This ain't the time to dwell on that.

The new goat bleats contentedly as I scratch her behind her ears. "Let's call this one Hopeful," I say to Ro. I like that, I like it a lot. But what I don't like is how quiet Tegan's being, as though she's got something to say but ain't quite sure how to say it. She's holdin' on to that last surprise, and fer a while, I think she'll take whatever it is and head back east with it.

I'll be sad to see 'em all go, but they've already brought us farther than they probably should have. It ain't legal fer any commoner to be in this Region, and besides, they have lives to git back to, not to mention illicit merchandise to transport across the continent.

I hug 'em all fiercely. They saved us. Tegan gave us this plan, this hope, and all three of 'em helped git us to this point, riskin' themselves countless times in the process.

"Tegan, I... I..." I got no words, fer once in my life. I've never felt so grateful to anyone before. All I cain do is hug her again.

"Don't mention it, Curlicue." She yanks on one of my locks. "I'll be back here in one year, and I expect the Captain to have something of tremendous value to offer me. You two gotta make that happen."

That's when the last secret comes spillin' out of her. They'd bought Hopeful from a trader-friendly merchant Tegan had dealt with years ago. Seems that merchant has loose lips.

"That business of theirs on the island, it was all the talk, I tell you." She pulls away from me so she cain address Ro as well. "Hush, hush talk, mind you, but still talk."

I don't know what she's goin' on about at first, but soon enough it becomes clear. "That merchant's been sellin' to a lot of the New Pioneer candidates. Most of 'em are as clueless as you'd expect, but a few of 'em seem to know what's what. On account of the information they was hintin' at, he suspects what's really happenin' on that island you're bound fer."

What it boils down to is this: us farmers is going to the island to grow food fer back home -- that's the official story. But unofficially, it's also to support some non-farmin' folk who'll be livin' on the island with us. This confirms to Tegan what she'd long suspected, that the hard work of makin' an island colony had to have a bigger aim aside from food production. She got the notion that we'll be makin' us a new edition of Ro's booklet durin' our first year there, one that includes everything that's in it so far plus some secrets the powers that be are sittin' on. I cain't help but be skeptical cuz she believes they're devising some kind of escape plan. This seems mighty far-fetched. It's probably just rumors them people was spreadin' and ain't nothin' more to it. Then I git to thinkin... wouldn't it make perfect rich-folk sense that they'd be workin' away at sich a thing in the middle of the ocean, thousands of miles away from the nearest desert-dweller?

If this planet comes to naught, who's the Council gonna see gits saved? And who's gonna be left behind to eat dirt and watch their children starve?

"If they're tryin' to figure a way of gittin' out of this reality into a better one, you cain't let them keep it a secret, Curlicue." She takes both of my shoulders and grips 'em. "Either everyone goes free or none of us do, you hear me?"

I nod, still unsure what to make of this new information. What do we focus on now, savin' this world, or figurin' out how to abandon it? And truly... will we be able to do either?

Tegan's grip lifts and she pulls me into yet another embrace. "No matter what, remember that I'm countin' on one hell of a trade next year."

She lets go of me, and Ro grasps her instead so he cain place something into her hands. "Why don't we start that particular trade right now?"

Tegan takes the copy of his booklet and runs her finger down its spine. "What if something happens to yer last one?"

"It doesn't matter. I've got a million copies stored right here." He taps his head and I recall how he recited perfectly the last page of his booklet fer us that day back at the cave.

She nods, then she hands him something as well. A slip of paper. "I don't know the Captain personally, only by reputation. But I trust what I've heard. He'll understand what this means. Give him this and you won't have no trouble gittin' on that ship."

With a final good-bye, the three traders head back out into the night, away from the saltwater air and pull of the ocean, back to where the dead and dyin', livin' and breathin', dust and dirt and wind and calm all meet in one dry land.

Ro is starin' at Tegan's last offerin'. I glance over, curious. "What's it say?"

He shows it to me, just four simple words:

They carry the truth.

Ch. 16: Trade

I'm standin' on a long pier next to Ro, wearin' black pants and a sturdy short sleeve blue shirt—the sensible kind of outfit a proper farmer would wear to work her prosperous Regions farm. Ro holds my arm, upright and stiff, wearin' similar garb procured fer us by Gina in a town fifty miles east of here. We need to look like we belong on that big tall ship at the end of the dock. I know exactly nothin' about boats, but Ro grew up in the capital, just up the hill from a port. He tells me the ship's a barquentine with three masts. The foremast is square-rigged, while the main and mizzen masts are fore-and-aft rigged. Whatever that all means. Honestly, I don't rightly care what kind of boat it is or which way its sails face as long as it gits me to that island.

It's a good ship fer makin' runs up and down the coast but evidently it cain handle a journey far out into the ocean as well. Ro takes it on faith that it's sea worthy, like it's a given that it cain keep us afloat and ain't no reason to doubt it. I shift on my feet, thinkin' about being' trapped on that thing fer weeks on end with nothin' but blue 'round me. My whole life I've wanted to be somewhere with an abundance of water. Guess I'm gittin' my wish and then some.

Ro squeezes my hand. Despite my protests, he's given me his medallion, the one only proper folks in the Regions is supposed to wear. I know without him havin' to say it that he'd do anything to git me on that boat, git me away from the danger he feels he's put me in. So we only got one medallion 'tween us, only one trinket provin' one person's Regions status, and Ro is determined it be me who puts it on display. Ain't no use arguing with him.

The line moves like it cain't grasp the concept that that's what lines is supposed to do. Looks like way more than the hundred-fifty people they're acceptin' as New Pioneers has shown up. Other folks ahead of us is turned away. We could be turned away. This could all still come to nothin'.

There's plenty of lawfolk here, too, which don't help my blood pressure none. It's probably standard, but I fear they're lookin' fer us. The half-covered flier in the boarding house bearin' Ro's likeness blows through my mind like dust across the plains. I bite my lip and give Ro another once over. He's wearin' a wide brimmed hat and his beard is all grown out again, fuller than it's ever been, he claims After months on the run, he's got harsher angles and a knowin' look in his eyes that don't reflect much upon that picture of him plastered all about town. Still, someone could surely recognize him. It ain't beyond reason'.

Slowly, we move up the line. Beads of sweat collect at the edge of my collar. "Come on, Nessie." I pull gently on her lead. Hopeful trails willingly in her shadow. It's a mighty consolation that I ain't gotta leave my Nessie behind, and gods willin', she'll live out the rest of her days without fearin' the bottom of a fryin' pan. She's all I have remainin' of the farm, my home fer the first nineteen years of my life. Even Frank's been left behind. Ain't no guns allowed in the Regions; gittin' caught with one would surely give us away. Vern's got Frank now. He'll give him a good home, no doubtin' that. But I cain't bear to think of Frank, tried and true friend of one May June Stebbins, bein' gone from my life, not when I gotta focus on my actin' skills. Cuz finally, we're up next.

We're questioned by some kind of official. She introduces herself as Ms. Portia. "And this is Captain Beatty." She points to an older man with a neatly trimmed mustache standin' behind her. He gives us a slight nod as Ms. Portia keeps talkin'. "We'll determine if you are eligible to become New Pioneers. If you are, you'll board immediately and be shown to your quarters."

"And if we're not eligible?" Ro tries to keep his words steady.

When she smiles, her lips practically disappear. "You needn't worry about that unless it's necessary. Your names please?"

We feed her the identities we've created fer ourselves. We're Christopher and April Stevens, newly married. I'm from a farmin' family in the Eastern Region. My husband's family owned a store in the nearest village. My family wanted me to wed another farmer but instead, I married Christopher here, and to avoid all of our parents' disapproval, we've decided to create a life together as New Pioneers. I do just as much talking as Ro, and if Ms. Portia thinks I ain't a genuine Regions lady, she don't show it.

"You have no farming skills?" Ms. Portia looks at Ro doubtfully. It's probably just me being paranoid, but she's starin' right at the part of Ro's chest where his medallion should be. Course he's got his vest buttoned up high, and ain't no way to tell his neck's bare under it, but I still cain't shake the feeling she's noted its absence. I wipe sweat on my pants, keep my smile loose like gittin' on this ship ain't the biggest deal of my life. Ms. Portia's eyes narrow. "Where did you say you were from again?"

Ro goes on about how much farmin' I've already taught him, which would be funny if our future didn't depend on him bein' believable. He tries to play on her emotions, talkin' 'bout how far we've traveled to git here. The Captain stares intently at Ro. Is he addin' things up? And if he is, is that a good thing?

Meanwhile, Ms. Portia has taken a dislikin' to us that ain't so subtle. She raises a hand like she's wavin' someone over. I clench my fists, fight the urge to turn around so I cain see who she's called. It's lawfolk. Gotta be. They're on to us, dang it! "We'd really prefer both parties to be experienced farmers, so I'm not-"

"May I please have a word with the Captain?" She don't take kindly to my interruption, but I ain't got much choice. "So sorry, I don't mean to be rude, but I believe my cousin's wife's father served with him years ago. Captain!" I call to him. "Do you remember someone named Lincoln Blakely?"

The Captain takes his hat off and scratches his head. No way cain he remember Lincoln Blakely since I just made him up myself. "I'm not sure that I-"

"He said to give you this." I offer him Tegan's paper. After a moment's pause, he takes it.

Ro holds his breath next to me, and Ms. Portia smiles her thin-as-a-shriveled-up-goat's-udder smile. Ain't no way she wants us on that boat. I count seven lawfolk within twenty feet of us and start calculatin' escape strategies. The person she called over a moment ago finally arrives at her side and she exchanges words with him. He ain't dressed like the other lawfolk, but that don't necessarily mean nothing'. Both of 'em cease their wisperin' so they cain gape at Ro. I ain't likin' where this is goin'.

Ro grasps me around the shoulders as we wait fer 'em to determine our fate. He rubs my arm and I cain't quite tell if it's to calm me or to keep himself from losin' it. If there was any more tension in the air, it'd be thicker than the dust storm that took out Callen.

Captain Beatty clears his throat, unfolds the paper and then folds it up again. "Lincoln Blakely." He shoves the paper into his coat pocket. "Of course, I remember him now. A fine man. How is... Matilda isn't it?"

"Why, she's wonderful! She and my cousin just had their third last winter. A girl this time." I widen my smile, make sure I'm lookin' pleased as punch at this exchange, and in truth, I am pleased. The Captain's playin' along. He don't have to do that, but he is.

He turns to Ms. Portia. "Mr. and Mrs. Stevens will be joining me on the Margarethe. Pass them through, Melanie."

Her face sours and she exchanges another look with her friend. Finally, that friend shrugs and takes a step back. He must be holdin' to the wise opinion that the Captain's word is final. Melanie Portia on the other hand, ain't gonna quit. "But, Captain, we have more candidates than we expected—well over three hundred. The Stevens simply aren't the best pioneers for this colony. Besides that, he-"

"Come along you two." Captain Beatty ignores her and motions us forward. Ms. Portia yammers on but I ain't focused on her no more cuz my brave, bold Ro just stuck out his hand for the Captain to shake. Beatty accepts it and holds it in his own fer a long while.

"Welcome aboard."

We got weeks upon weeks of seafarin' ahead of us. All we do at first is git settled in, earn our sea legs. The Captain don't ask us fer more details right away, but he knows, I cain tell. He knows who Ro is. It's plain as day from the way his eyes slide toward us every time our paths cross his on the decks of the Margarethe.

Four days into our voyage, bellies rollin' with the sea, blue as Ro's eyes all 'round us, dreams of brown as the fertile world waitin' fer us on a distant island, Captain Beatty invites us to dine with him in his fancy quarters. Alone. This gives me an occasion to wear Ma's silver hair clip, as well as a reason to send my stomach turnin' more than the waves ever could.

"The port was crawling with officers," he says 'fore I've even had the opportunity to pick up my fork. "You were lucky to have escaped."

"I don't know what-" Ro starts, but the captain holds up a hand to silence him.

"You carry the truth." He takes Tegan's crumpled bit of paper and waves it at us. "The truth is all I've ever wanted."

I knew this was comin', I been waitin' fer this moment. Ro looks to me, and I nod. He slips the last copy of Why the Spread of the Desert Should Matter to You out of his coat and hands it to him.

Captain Beatty takes it in one hand and brings the other up to his eyes, rubbin' like he needs to polish 'em, like that'll somehow convince himself that the booklet is real. Finally, he just says, "My gods."

Ro tells him our story best we cain, and then I say: "We'll need paper." I draw out my 'a' the way I grew up doin'. Ain't gotta hide behind a fake accent no more, not with him. "Our friend thought you'd be able to supply us with some. And while we're at it, how about you tell us a truth we've been wantin' to hear. Just what is goin' on on that island we're headed to? And if you say it ain't nothin' more than growin' pineapples and rice, I may have to snatch Ro's booklet back from you and start a dang mutiny."

\#

The Captain ain't no ignorant Regions farmer comin' to plow the tropical isle, no thought as to why he's doin' it. He's a trader like Tegan, when you think of it, only more on the up and up as far as most proper people are aware of. He's been haulin' goods along the west coast fer a generation, even gittin' a commendation last spring fer all his years of service. But unbeknownst to the Council, Captain Beatty is a lot more like Tegan and her lot than he would appear to be.

Don't matter to Beatty if what he carries has got the Council's stamp of approval on it or not. If he thinks it serves the people – all of the people – he's gonna' transport it. That's why we're on this ship rather than on one populated with lawfolk in route to a jail in the capital. He believes Ro serves the people. And damned if that Captain ain't gonna git his Council-unapproved merchandise to where it cain do some good.

As fer what the Captain suspects about the true purpose of the island, well, he ain't supposed to know a thing, of course. Granddad used to say that "supposed to" and "in actuality" ain't always a match, and lucky fer us, that's the case this time 'round. The Captain is a solid sort, meanin' people tend to look upon him as a man who cain be trusted. Since fer all them proper folks know he's a loyal, upstandin' Regions citizen, they tend to spill more to him than Granddad would to the bartender after a couple of pints.

"For your own good," he cautions us, "you have to be careful how you approach these people. You need to win their friendship first, get them to tell you what it is they're really doing."

Who "these people" are is a small group of science-minded folks who believe the secret of opening a portal out of this world has been hidden away on our new island paradise. Supposedly, it's been there just about since the first pioneers found themselves stranded on this hunk of rock. Disguised as New Pioneers, these scientists have been charged by the Council with findin' that secret and learnin' how to make use of it. Supposedly the aim is to git out some kind of distress signal to other realities, lettin' 'em know we're still here and need their help.

I'm thinkin' though, that Tegan weren't too far off in her assessment that the Council is goin' to use the island's secrets to save their own sorry asses. She's right: we gotta make sure that whatever gits discovered is shared with every last unlucky person on this planet. And Captain Beatty's right too: we need to proceed with caution. Not even he knows fer certain the identities of all of those supposed secret-gatherers. He gives us the name of the two he's purdy dang sure about, a couple who traveled to the island on Beatty's last voyage there.

"Well ain't that perfect." I twist a lock of curls 'round my finger. "They got the jump start on us already."

Captain Beatty chuckles. He likes me, I cain tell. Not in the gross I-wanna-gag way of Orin and his pa, but in a fatherly-type way. It's more wholesome than I know what to do with. "They aren't necessarily the enemy, my dear. Just don't count them as friends yet either. Their loyalties, like yours, lie in finding the truth, but for what purpose they'll use that truth when it's discovered is impossible to decipher."

"If anyone is able to judge a person's character and determine what their intentions are, it's May." Ro places an arm around my waist; his fingers play with the belt loop on my trousers.

"Well that's the truth all right. I figured you out purdy much before you ever set foot on my farm." This ain't strictly true, but he don't ever have to know it.

The Captain laughs again, but then he takes on a more serious expression, like the one he always wears when he's givin' his chief officer an order. "You probably have found little to love about this world."

I wouldn't have hesitating in confirmin' this notion 'fore I met Ro, but now I gotta reevaluate. "Well, there is certainly truth in that, sir. But, like Ro here, I think I've come to an understandin' with it. I've been grieved by this world. It's been the source of much sufferin', mine and others. But it's givin' me life, too, I cain't ferget that. I don't wanna see it die."

"Nor do I." He's starin' out of the porthole, the darkest blue of night with a million pin pricks of light starin' back at him. "This world, this land, even the ocean, it's been made by the people who've lived and died here. We make it what we dream it to be. And we've had our fair share of nightmares."

The captain may be waxin' all poetic, but I gotta nod in agreement, cuz this is so much like what I've thought myself on many occasions, about the dust at least. The dust is the people. It exists cuz we do. "Do you believe the world has a spirit, sir?"

Captain Beatty turns away from the porthole so he cain see if I'm askin' my question in all sincerity. Ro knows I am. He's sittin' with his chair tilted back. The hours we just spent eatin' and discussing the state of the world with Beatty seems to have made him as comfortable as if he was dinin' at my table back at the farm.

The captain takes his time before answerin'. "It must be so. It's alive isn't it?"

"Fer now." I git up and step around the table, headin' over to peer out the porthole just as the captain had done. "We got ourselves an understandin', Captain, cuz I know it has a spirit, too, and that spirit is but one and the same with our own. We dreamed this world alive, as you say. It's alive cuz we are, and we're alive cuz of it. Good or bad, that's a connection we cain't take fer granted."

Ro sits up quick, his chair thunkin' down as he lands with his hands on the table in front of him. "So what happens if the world can't be saved? What happens if our only hope of survival is to find a way off of it?"

Well, that's the same question I've been askin' myself ever since Tegan seeded it in my mind. There ain't no way fer me to have an answer to it, though, not now. "Last I checked, I ain't got no crystal ball. I guess we gotta find out fer ourselves."

Ch. 17: Verge

Captain Beatty supplies us with more than just paper and ink. There is indeed something aside from vegetable growin' goin' on on this island we're headin' to; thanks to Beatty, we got an idea of who to cozy up to fer information about that. These are people who carry secrets just like we do. Only theirs is a might more unbelievable, if you ain't acquainted with the particulars. Accordin' to whoever blabbed to Beatty, somewhere on this dusty world of ours lies the most fertile seed of hope you cain imagine; thousand year-old formulas and computations that cain open a channel back to other realities.

I ain't givin' up on this reality, though, and neither is Ro. We're gonna fight fer it like you wouldn't believe, but that fight has gotta include learnin' what these island scientists figured out regardin' a means of escape. And who knows? There's gotta be some smart people in one of them other parallel planes. If we cain't fix our problems, maybe some genius from another universe cain. I know Tegan had her doubts regardin' whether these scientists are really just aimin' to git us some outside help. She's earned her cynicism the way all of us desert dwellers have, through hard livin' and experience. But the idea that there's someone who cain help our world just waitin' fer us to ask fer it does have its appeal. Maybe we don't gotta do this alone. Maybe our salvation lies beyond this world in one we cain't neither see nor quite conceive of.

Beatty believes in this, says some of the original pioneers knew how to journey to other realms, as he calls 'em. The story goes that they hid that knowledge somewhere fer safe-keepin' cuz they firmly believed that no one should try to leave, that we was destined fer this reality and this reality only. Why these scientists think that hidin' place is on our island is anyone's guess.

Have them scientists found what they're lookin' fer yet? Are they already studyin' them old pioneer texts? We gotta find out. We gotta understand what's goin' on so we cain represent the world: lucky and unlucky folks, the desert, the Regions. Everyone. Everywhere. We gotta see that there ain't one spirit fergotten about if they find a way to high-tale it out of here.

'Fore we dock at our new home, Beatty gives us a note just as Tegan had done. It's to be used if we feel one of those scientists cain be trusted. If none of 'em cain, we gotta be like spies, infiltrate their operation just like we did to git on this ship. I am hopin' so hard that we cain find at least one trustworthy person among the lot. It would be nice to have us an ally.

I run my fingers over the captain's note, trustin' that I won't have to keep it hidden ferever. He's written almost the exact same thing Tegan had on hers:

Their truth is your own. Make it the world's.

\#

We arrive in our island paradise and we git to work. We are New Pioneers in a manner that the council in their stuffy capital towers thousands of miles away ain't never thought of before. We are pioneering a new way of thinkin', a new way of seein'.

We are pioneers of hope.

Sometimes I think back to them early days—meetin' Ro, leavin' home, survivin' all sorts of perils, all to bring us to this tropical land that couldn't even imagine a desert if it tried. It all seems like a fantastical dream. At night, when I lay with my head on Ro's chest, I wonder if I'm not really back at the farm—that a dust storm didn't just appear one day instead of a handsome stranger and bury me under a hundred years of dried-up hope.

I am here, though, alive and whole. Ro's heartbeat poundin' steady under my ear confirms that fer me. His eyes tell me everything when they search fer mine... when he looks to me to write the next chapter of our story. This is how I know hope ain't dried-up. It's alive as long as we are, as long as we continue on. And so is this world.

All my life, I saw the desert as a demon, trappin' every unlucky person who came within its reach. But those weeks on the run with Ro taught me something more—that every person cain change her luck, no matter how unlikely it may seem. The desert cain be made an ally, cain even be an angel of mercy if you wake it real gentle and tell it yer deepest desires.

The world cain change its course, and even if it refuses, the people cain change theirs.

Ro and me, we got us a lifetime to change the luck of the world the same way we transformed our own. Shortly after arrivin' here, I mentioned to Ro how crazy his 'round-about trip through the land had been. He could've caught a boat south from the capital, been to the port town in a couple of weeks and hid until the ship to the island set sail. Instead, he nearly died several times over again, crossin' every which way, walkin' over a thousand miles till he finally found himself back on the coast.

"I'd do it all over again." He pulls me close, kisses me long and deep. "Every single mile. It's all a small price to pay in order to have found you, May."

It's the journey that matters. It's what you find along the way. It's how you keep goin' even when the most rational part of you knows you should quit. You don't lay down in the street and let yerself be carried away. You keep goin'. You always, always endure.

This is what we do now. This is how we endure. When we ain't farmin' this rich earth, we're makin' friends with the captain's suspected scientists, carefully sussin' out what they know, what they've discovered, if there truly is anything to discover here. And when we ain't doin' that, we're writin'—writin' out Ro's booklet again and again, hopin' to add to it a new truth: there is a way to survive this world, even if the world itself is to die. There are countless realities out there and there's a way to open the door to them realities. Somehow. Somewhere.

We write with the knowledge that we are privileged to be able to do so. Each word is a mile in the wilderness, a remembrance of what it took and the lives lost to git us here. This is our promise to those lives, and to the desert that spared us ours. The lucky and the unlucky, the rich and the poor, the desert and the fertile lands and the ocean, the whole world—it's just on the verge of an awakenin'.

All we need to do is shake it gently, and fill its mind with the truth.